Dear Reader,

I spent free time on a relative's farm when I was growing up. The bull with a ring in his nose who resided in the pasture had traveled all the way from Texas to Pennsylvania! I spun stories in my head about the ranch he'd come from and the cowboys there. Texas has always held allure for me.

When I began writing *Love, Honor and a Pregnant Bride*, I immediately fell in love with my hero Jud Whitmore— one of those Texas cowboys. He is an honorable, duty-bound man who can't admit a woman has stolen his heart. When Mariah turns up on his family's ranch pregnant… Well, if a marriage of convenience doesn't transform this recalcitrant cowboy into a perfect husband, maybe Mariah's love will do the trick.

I hope this romance gives my readers a rewarding taste of happily-ever-after!

All my best,

Karen Rose Smith

GREATEST TEXAS LOVE STORIES OF ALL TIME

GREATEST
TEXAS LOVE STORIES
OF ALL TIME

LOVE, HONOR AND A PREGNANT BRIDE
Karen Rose Smith

He's a Cowboy!

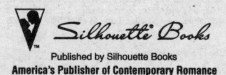

Silhouette Books

Published by Silhouette Books

America's Publisher of Contemporary Romance

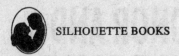

SILHOUETTE BOOKS

RECYCLED PAPER

ISBN 0-373-65223-2

LOVE, HONOR AND A PREGNANT BRIDE

Copyright © 1998 by Karen Rose Smith

Visit Silhouette at www.eHarlequin.com

Printed in U.S.A.

KAREN ROSE SMITH

began reading romances as a teenager. Her favorites included horses. Farms, ranches and the beautiful intuitive animals still beckon to her now that she's an adult. She insists the peace she can find in these settings can't be matched anywhere. She will never pass up the chance to pet and talk to a horse or walk into a barn and smell the wonderful scents of hay, horses and leather! She called up memories from childhood experiences on a relative's farm to create the Star Four, the setting for Jud and Mariah's romance. Karen Rose likes to hear from her readers. You can write to her c/o Silhouette Books, 233 Broadway, Suite 1001, NY, NY 10279 or through her Web site at www.karenrosesmith.com.

Books by Karen Rose Smith

Silhouette Romance

Silhouette Special Edition

Silhouette Books

Previously published under the pseudonym Kari Sutherland

Silhouette Romance

Silhouette Special Edition

To all those who helped me with research on Texas, cutting horses and cowboys: Eve, Kristi, Roxanne, Roz, Rusty and Threasa. And to Kathy and Tim, who let me experience the joy of pastures, barns and horses again.

Prologue

"**J.T.** What's wrong?"

Mariah Roswell's soft voice skittered up his spine the same way her hands had a few moments before. He'd never felt so much, or dreamed so much, or shaken so much as he had in that moment when the two of them had become one. But it had been an impulse, a mistake, a disaster...and it had been *wrong*.

As she shifted against him under the saddle blanket that he'd hastily pulled over them to protect her from Montana's February cold, he glimpsed her small breasts and wanted her all over again. "Dammit, Mariah, this never should have happened. You're a twenty-one-year-old virgin. I'm ten years older than you. And to let it happen unprotected to boot..."

"I *was* a virgin," she told him with a smile that was part remembered innocence, part pride.

Although he wanted to roll her over on her back and sink into her again, he knew better. After his last argument with his father, he'd left Texas and the Star Four over a year ago and intended never to look back. He'd told himself he'd find his own dream, lasso it, and ride with it. Only the dream had escaped him. He'd become a drifter, ending up on this ailing cattle spread in Montana a month ago.

Mariah was the housekeeper's daughter, and he should have kept his distance. But with her dark auburn hair and her green eyes, with her skills with a mustang and her lilting voice, he'd been intrigued, entranced and at times downright stymied. And from the first moment their eyes had met, his Stetson had felt too loose, his boots too tight and the rest of him as hot as a Texas summer.

She reached out, tenderly stroking his jaw, and said, "Don't look so worried, J.T."

Then he *did* roll her over on her back in the straw, not to make love to her again but to get her attention. "This isn't some romantic dream, Mariah. I'm going to be gone as fast as I arrived and—"

The sound of the barn door opening had him scrambling to his feet, sliding into his jeans and boots, and buttoning his shirt quicker than lightning could strike.

He'd pulled the blanket over Mariah, motioning her

to keep silent when he heard the top hand call, "J.T.? You in here? Ya got a phone call."

"Right here, Chip."

He left the empty stall and hurried down the ground walk-through so the cowhand wouldn't come any closer and find Mariah. "Are you sure it's for me?" Nobody knew his whereabouts except his two cousins Luke and Christopher. He knew he could trust them.

"The man, a Mr. Langston, says it's some kind of emergency. You'd better git to the bunkhouse fast."

Christopher. If anything had happened to Luke... Even as his thoughts scrambled, he remembered Mariah and the need to protect her. "You'd better come with me, Chip. In case I have to...get the truck started up in the cold."

"You goin' somewhere?"

"I hope not. But an emergency isn't usually good news." He had a sinking feeling in his gut about this call, and he hoped to God he was wrong.

Chapter One

The evening sun streaked the horizon with orange and pink as Mariah sat on the porch swing with a magazine for a few quiet moments before she turned in. She didn't need quite as much sleep now as she had the first three months of her pregnancy. But she still made sure she got plenty of rest...for the baby's sake.

It had been four months since she'd made love to J.T. in the barn. And although he'd left that night for some emergency he'd never explained to her or anyone else, she didn't regret what had happened. She'd never really felt like a woman until J.T. had driven his dusty truck onto the ranch where her mother had settled them ten years ago. She'd always been a part of the scenery here. Taken for granted. Considered one of the "fellas" to the boys she'd grown up with. Considered a child by the owner of the ranch and her mother and Chip.

But when J.T. had arrived, everything had changed. The rakish cowboy with the crooked smile and no last name had stolen her heart.

She would have contacted him about the baby, but he'd signed on as a temporary hand, asked for a cash salary and had volunteered nothing about his background. All of that should have warned her to stay away. But something in his blue eyes, as well as the restlessness in his soul, had beckoned to her like a rainbow inviting her to find the pot of gold.

She patted her tummy. She'd found the pot of gold, all right.

With a sigh, she flipped through the glossy pages of the magazine with more intent than interest until a photo sat in her lap that made her breath catch.

It was J.T.!

Wasn't it?

The photograph had been taken on the Star Four Ranch in Texas. She read the caption underneath. "Thatcher Whitmore hands the reins of the Star Four to his son Jud." As Mariah scanned the article, she learned that J.T. was Judson Thatcher Whitmore, heir to the Star Four, a ranch outside of Tyler that bred and trained cutting horses. The elder Whitmore had suffered a heart attack in February and had turned over management of the nationally known and re-

spected ranch to his son. The article went on to quote
Thatcher Whitmore and his expectations now that the
ranch was in his son's hands. There were no quotes
from Jud.

Mariah studied the picture more closely. Jud's face
bore the same rugged lines and angles as J.T.'s, his
legs were as long, his shoulders as broad. But
Thatcher Whitmore's son had lost the amused twinkle
in his blue eyes under the brim of his Stetson. There
was no hint of the smile that could be seductive and
boyish at the same time. More was different about the
cowboy she'd fallen in love with than just his name.

She'd told herself over the past few months that he
would contact her if she'd meant anything to him.
Yet, now, staring at his face, knowing his father's
heart attack had been the emergency that had taken
him away, her sense of fairness won over her pride.

Judson Thatcher Whitmore deserved to know he'd
fathered a child.

Hopping off the swing, Mariah hurried inside. She
found her mother sitting in their bedroom in a rocking
chair, staring out the window. Edda Roswell was only
fifty, but her hair was mostly gray now. They'd lived
on the Hopkins ranch for ten years, since her father's
fatal bull-riding accident. His death had left them in
debt for the funeral, let alone other bills he'd racked
up in between his winnings. Edda had taken the job
as housekeeper for Jethro Hopkins to give them a

place to live, using the only skills she had—cooking and cleaning.

Mariah couldn't contain her excitement as she crossed to her mother quickly, kneeling beside her. "Look what I found, Mama."

Edda Roswell took the magazine, glanced at it and looked up. "Seems to me you didn't know J.T. very well. What are you gonna do?"

"I'm going to him. I have some money saved." Besides helping her mother and working with Chip whenever he'd let her, she took in sewing. She'd been putting everything they didn't need aside for the baby.

"There's something you oughtta know," her mother said softly. "Mr. Hopkins is thinking about selling out. This was a rough winter. He lost about twenty-five head, not counting the new calves that didn't make it."

"No. He can't sell! Where would you go?"

"Honey, I'm fit. I can get a job keeping house for someone else, or cooking or waitressing if it comes down to it. But I'm worried about you and the baby. The trip. Wasting your money. What if J.T. doesn't care he got you pregnant?"

Her mother had liked J.T. well enough when he was a hand. But the fact he'd left her with child.... Yet Mariah had sensed a deep-down strength in J.T. that she believed wouldn't let him turn away from his offspring.

"He'll care. I know he will. I'm going to pack and

ask Chip to drive me to Billings. Then I'm catching a bus and heading for Texas.'' She saw the worry on her mother's face and gave her a hug. ''Everything will be fine, Mama. I know it.''

With all her might, Mariah believed her trip to Texas would bring her happiness...and a father for her baby.

Mariah hiked up the road to the Star Four Monday afternoon, hot, tired and dusty. Her jeans stuck to the back of her knees and she wished she'd worn her sneakers instead of boots on the last leg of the bus ride. But she wasn't going to stop in the middle of nowhere to change them now.

When she'd seen the wooden arch and the carved symbol of the Star Four, she'd made the taxi driver stop there, not wanting to put any more money out for the fare than she had to. But she hadn't expected the road to the ranch to be so long. She'd walked at least half a mile, scanning the brush, the black-eyed Susans, the sweet gums and oaks in the distance, the miles of well-tended fence. So different from where she'd grown up. Yet fascinating in its way.

After another quarter of a mile, her stomach got queasy. She hadn't eaten since the crackers she'd munched on midmorning and it was now at least two. As she kept walking, she took in the brick house across the road from barns, corrals and outbuildings, one of them large enough to be an indoor arena. With a woman's radar, she spotted J.T. immediately in one of the corrals. She'd recognize the long legs, broad shoulders and tilt of his hat anywhere. Switching her duffel to her left hand because her trek had made it seem heavier than it was, she headed for the corral and J.T.

But when she reached the fence, he'd gone inside the barn. The sun blazing hot on her head, she thought more about purpose than about what she was going to say. After unhitching the corral gate, she walked through the open barn door, hearing voices. She soon saw a horse trailer parked at the back of the barn. The rear door, big enough for the truck to drive through, was also open.

"I'll call the vet and get him checked out." J.T.'s voice, its remembered depth and low pitch, resounded through her like a favorite song.

"Shelby's not going to be happy if you can't start working him right away," an older man warned.

Mariah recognized him from the picture. He was Thatcher Whitmore. He, too, wore jeans, boots and a Stetson. But his shirt was clean, his silver belt buckle shiny, his boots not crusted with dry earth like J.T.'s. As tall as J.T. and just as broad shouldered, he seemed twice as big, his chest wider, his stomach thick over his belt. He was a robust man with the authority in his tone to match his build.

"I'll handle Shelby," J.T. answered flatly.

"Yeah, just watch *how* you handle her. She wants more than havin' her horse worked."

At J.T.'s low oath, Mariah took a few steps forward. "J.T.?"

The barn didn't carry all the heat of the outdoors, but as J.T.'s gaze met hers, she felt as if she could go up in flames as easy as the dry hay in the stall beside her. For a moment she thought she saw a flicker of joy, maybe even the desire they had tried to deny but couldn't resist. Then it was gone with a curt question. "What are you doing here?"

"Who the hell is J.T.?" Thatcher demanded.

She dropped her duffel bag and both men's eyes went to it as if it was a rattler about to strike. "Can I talk to you privately?" she asked the cowboy whose friendly smiles had been much different than his present attitude.

"Anything that's got to be said can be said right here," the older man concluded as he stuck out his hand. "Thatcher Whitmore. And you are…"

She let his large beefy fingers envelop hers and gave them a firm shake. "Mariah Roswell. I have some business with your son. I only knew him as J.T. He didn't have a last name when he worked in Montana."

"Business, is it?" Thatcher asked, his gaze giving her a thorough inspection before settling on her duffel bag again. "Looks like the kind of business I should know about. Especially since my boy seems to have taken an alias. You hate the Whitmore name and me so much, you couldn't use it when you were gone?" he asked his son tersely.

J.T. took a step forward then, the lines on his face deeper than they'd been in February. She knew him well enough to see a retort form in his mind, but he pursed his lips and looked as if he was counting to ten. "Miss Roswell said her business is with me. Why don't you go up to the house and rest. Get Flo to give you one of those sugar-free cookies she baked."

Thatcher's face reddened. "Just because I gave you authority over the books doesn't mean you can tell me what to do. I want to know what's goin' on. And I'm not leavin' till I find out what this young lady has to say."

J.T.'s jaw tensed with anger. "Fine."

Both men were waiting for her to speak. Knowing this was *not* the best way of telling J.T., but having no choice, she took a deep breath. "I'm pregnant."

She never knew a barn could be so silent. Even the horse behind J.T. didn't twitch his tail or lift his head. Mariah waited for an explosion.

Instead of an explosion, Thatcher Whitmore let out a booming laugh. "I'll be damned. You *were* busy while you were away, Son. Nothing I'd like more than to be a grandpa."

"That's it!" J.T. growled. Taking Mariah's arm firmly in his grasp, he propelled her to the front of the barn and out the door, leaving his father chuckling in the background. She saw two cowhands who were hauling bales from the back of a pickup truck into another barn glance at her curiously.

J.T. didn't stop until they stood at least twenty yards from the barn door under the shade of a pecan tree. "Bad enough I have to coddle him and can't speak my mind, let alone take care of the books and supervise the work, too. Now you turn up here claiming to be pregnant—"

"I'm not *claiming* to be pregnant. I *am* pregnant." She didn't know what kind of reception she'd expected, but to be considered just another of life's stresses sparked her temper.

His blue gaze raked over her. "You don't *look* pregnant."

In her plaid blouse and jeans, she supposed that was true. With the nausea she'd experienced, she'd actually lost weight the first few months of her pregnancy. The changes to her body were still subtle, but they were there. "Would you like me to take off my clothes? I'm sure you'd find a couple of differences. Unless, of course, you don't remember."

The nerve in his jaw worked. "Remember? What should I remember? That we had a quick but literal roll in the hay?"

Blame it on hormones, blame it on wishing for a dream, but his hastily flung questions brought tears to her eyes. If that's all she was to him, she shouldn't be here. This man wasn't the cowboy she'd fallen in love with. He was a stranger. Not wanting him to see how much he'd hurt her, she spun away. If it weren't for the money it would cost to replace the vitamins in her duffel bag, she'd head for the road rather than the barn.

But she'd only managed a couple of feet before he caught her elbow. "Mariah."

She didn't know what she heard in his voice. It was less than anger, more than frustration.

When she tried to yank away, he held her fast. "Are you sure it's mine?"

That did it. The tears burned away into a flare of temper she didn't know she possessed. "Oh, I'm sure, all right. Seeing as I was a virgin when you…slept with me, and I had morning sickness so badly right after so as I couldn't look at food much less want to keep company with a man. I'm very certain it's yours!"

He released her and tipped up the brim of his hat. "I had to make sure."

"The only way you'll have proof is to get a DNA test done after the baby's born. If that's what it takes, that's what we'll do."

Studying her with an intensity that was new and as disconcerting as the devil, he said, "There won't be a need. I believe you're telling me the truth."

"I want to know why you didn't tell *me* the truth," she returned, still stung by his initial reaction.

His face darkened. "I never lied about anything. I

told you you were too young for me. I told you I'd be leaving.''

"You kept your name from me, your background, your life. I thought you were some penniless drifter until I saw the picture of you and your father—''

With a step that was menacingly close, he asked in a voice low in timbre but loud in purpose, "Did you come here for money?''

Thoughts of all the needs for the baby ran neck in neck with her desire to see J.T. and touch him again. "I didn't come here to blackmail you.''

"But if you hadn't seen that article, would you have tried to find me?''

"Thank God I *did* see it. How else would I have found you? Or was that your intent? Maybe I'm not the first woman in this spot. How many more women did you sleep with when you were pretending to be a cowboy with no last name?'' Her fervor and the desperate need to know the answer to her question made her dizzy.

Jud closed his eyes for a moment against the rush of regret and self-recriminations that had been galloping through his mind since the night he'd taken Mariah's virginity. He'd thought he'd taken her innocence, too, but now he wasn't so sure. She might have come for another reason than to tell him he was a father. She might be after a bankbook of Whitmore money or a stake in the Star Four. He'd seen women, time and time again, go after what his father possessed rather than the man he was. One particular woman who Thatcher had made his fiancée came immediately to mind. Thanks to heaven, Jud had found her cheating on his father with one of the hands a week before the wedding.

Thatcher had pitched a fit, claiming Jud had lied because he didn't get on with the "lady." But there had been more than one hand who owed loyalty to his dad rather than some woman who only cared what the master of the Star Four could buy her. And all the dirty laundry had been brought out into the light.

Jud's own experience with women had led him to believe what he owned was more important than the man he was. Suddenly he wished he could remember his mother—as much as he wished he'd resisted Mariah. He hadn't even had the inclination to stand close to another woman since he'd been with this green-eyed virgin.

"J.T.? Answer me," she demanded.

Her demand broke the patience he'd been losing his grip on since he'd been called home in February. "The name is Jud," he snapped. "And I don't owe you any explanations. If you came here expecting me to welcome you with open arms—" Seeing how her complexion had faded from an overheated rosy to pale, he nudged her chin up in his palm. "What's wrong?"

"I don't...feel very well."

Sweat broke out on her brow and as her knees

started to buckle, he swept her up in his arms, swearing as he quickly carried her across the road to the house.

Barging through the door with her, the screen door slapping behind him, he called to the woman who had dusted him off and patched him up more than a few times while he was growing up. "Flo, bring in a glass of water. And a cold cloth." His boots sounded on the wood floor as he carried Mariah to the sofa and set her down against the rough fabric. The air-conditioned house should cool her off, but he wasn't taking any chances.

"How did you get here?" he asked gruffly.

She struggled to pull herself up against the wide arm of the sofa patterned in desert colors. "Bus."

"Then what?"

"A cab," she muttered. "He let me off at the arch—"

Jud swore again, harder and longer. "Don't you have any sense? That's a mile hike and in this heat…"

"But I didn't know it would be a mile, did I? It's not as if I had a cell phone and a number I could call," she returned with spirit, though her face was still much too pale.

"Flo?" Jud bellowed. Wanting to kiss Mariah and shake her at the same time, he said, "You could have called from town."

"And what if you weren't here? What if you didn't want to talk to me?"

How many times had he wanted to call her over the past few months? Too many to count. But he'd figured it was better for her and him if he didn't. Lord knew he had enough of everything else taking up his time and his energy.

Flo rushed in with a tall glass in one hand, a towel in the other. "Get her boots off and she'll cool down quicker."

His hands went to Mariah's right boot. But before he could pull, she sat up, her hands covering his. He felt the heat of her fingers, her soft skin, and his body remembered every touch and every pleasure he'd taken with her. Their eyes met, and his throat went as dry as an August with no rain.

He thought a little color came back to her cheeks when she finally said, "I can do it myself."

One thing he admired about Mariah was her I-can-do-anything attitude. But there was a time and place for it, and that time and place wasn't now. "But I can do it faster." Before she could protest, he'd yanked the boot from one foot, then the other.

"J.T.," she warned.

"Jud," he reminded and took the glass from Flo. "Here, drink it slow." Taking the towel from the housekeeper, he said, "Flo, this is Mariah Roswell. She'll be visiting for a while. Flo keeps the house in shape and her husband Mack tries to keep my father from having another heart attack. They've been part of the Star Four since before I was born.''

"She'll be doin' more than visitin','' Thatcher announced from the doorway. "The two of you are gettin' hitched.''

Discreetly Flo went back to the kitchen as Jud clamped the lid on his anger. This was exactly the reason he'd left the Star Four for a year to find his own life. Maybe he should have left again after his dad was feeling better. Maybe he should have let Mack become the one in charge. Trying to keep stress to a minimum for Thatcher was causing him headaches of his own.

Though he wanted to shout for his father to mind his own business, he instead said, "Don't interfere, Dad.''

"I'll damned well interfere if I want. No grandchild of mine is gonna be runnin' around someplace without the Whitmore name.''

Jud took a deep breath and laid the cloth against Mariah's forehead as he counted to twenty. "If you want me to stay here, you'll have to keep out of my private affairs.''

It was as close to an ultimatum as he'd ever come with his father. But with Mariah here, they needed a definite understanding. Jud would not tolerate Thatcher running his life.

"You're gonna do the right thing by her.''

As Mariah put her own hand to the towel, Jud faced

his father toe-to-toe as calmly as he could. "*I* will decide what's right. *I* will decide what I want."

"Well, I'll be waitin' for that day. But if it takes too long, I'll get the preacher myself."

Mariah took the cloth from her forehead. "Mr. Whitmore, I won't marry J.T., um, Jud, if he doesn't want to marry me."

Thatcher rolled his eyes. "*Two* stubborn young 'uns. Just what I need."

"Mr. Whitmore," she tried again. "Jud and I haven't had a chance to talk about any of this. I'm sure it's as much of a shock to him as it is to you and…"

"Darlin', it's no shock. It's a blessing. And just call me Thatcher. You want time to talk, I'll give you time to talk, but the end result's gonna be the same." He winked at her. "Don't you worry none. He'll come around." With that, Thatcher followed Flo to the kitchen.

Jud knew if he let go of his self-restraint now, he'd blow the roof off the house.

"You and your father don't get along?" Mariah asked softly.

She had the power to arouse him and the power to calm him. That's what he'd found fascinating about her in addition to unsettling. The calm washed over him with her voice and her gently curious question. "Oh, we get along just fine. As long as we're on different sections." His father wasn't a subject he wanted to tackle with her still looking pale.

"When did you leave home?" he asked, taking the cloth from her hands and again holding it to her forehead. She didn't protest, and he realized whatever energy she'd used to make this trip had faded with her trek in the heat.

"Yesterday," she murmured.

"And when did you eat last?"

"Around ten."

He gave her a hard look. "That's no way to take care of yourself and a baby."

Brushing his hand and the towel away, she glared at him. "I ran out. I got hungrier than I expected last night and ate the apple and peanut butter crackers I was supposed to have for lunch."

Seeing her embarrassment at the admission, he couldn't help but tease. "Gain any weight yet?"

"You apparently didn't notice any," she tossed back, then took a few more swallows of water. Not able to help himself, he lodged on the sofa beside her hip, his thigh brushing against her. He'd been stunned to see her standing in the barn, thrown for a wide loop by what she'd had to say. As he studied her now more carefully, he *could* see subtle changes. Her hair was longer, her cheeks a bit fuller, and her breasts... He could see the outline of her bra through the blouse.

"I notice," he responded, wanting to slip her blouse buttons out of their holes, wanting to hold her breasts in his palms to see exactly how they'd changed.

Electricity vibrated between them until he said, "I'll ask Flo to make you a sandwich or two. Then you can go upstairs and rest." As he reminded himself she might be after money or a chunk of the Star Four rather than a father for her child, he stood and crossed to the doorway.

"J.T." She stopped and seemed to remind herself again of his real name. "Jud. We haven't talked about what's going to happen...."

"There's nothing to talk about. You're staying until the baby's born. In the meantime, I've got work to do. Don't you move until Flo calls you. And down that glass. Everyone here is going to make sure you take care of yourself so you might as well get used to it."

Seeing her mouth open, he knew she was going to give him her two cents worth. Well, he didn't want it right now. He had work to do and not enough time in the day to do it. He was through the kitchen and out the door when he decided he'd better fit some thinking in, too. Because Mariah Roswell, with the news she'd brought him, was a lot more difficult to maneuver than a schedule to train horses.

Chapter Two

Crumbs from two sturdy sandwiches stood on Mariah's plate as she finished a glass of lemonade.

"If you keep eating like that, you and the baby will be just fine," Flo said from her position at the sink where she was squeezing lemons for another batch of lemonade. It was the first she'd spoken to Mariah except to tell her lunch was ready.

"I hope so," Mariah answered. She'd only regained her appetite about a week or so ago. Before that she'd only managed food for the good of the baby.

"Just don't you go trying to save your figure. You'll only hurt the little one."

Little one. Mariah liked thinking of her child in those terms. She gently rubbed her stomach. "I wouldn't do anything to hurt this baby. I love him already. I can't wait to feel some movement."

Flo stopped pushing the half of lemon on the squeezer. "You have a mama?"

Mariah nodded.

"What's she think about all this?"

Mariah had always trusted her instincts with people. Already she sensed a solid feeling from Flo and guessed the housekeeper wasn't asking out of idle curiosity. "She's worried about me. And the baby."

"And right she should be. You landed smack dab in a pen with two bulls ready to charge each other."

"You mean Jud and his father?"

"Yep. And it looks to me like you're gonna end up in the middle of the fray. You up to it?"

"I'm going to do what's best for my baby no matter what either of them says or wants. And that might mean leaving. I won't stay if Jud doesn't want the baby or if Mr. Whitmore tries to use me to make Jud do something he doesn't want."

Where before Flo's expression had been noncommittal, now she smiled. "A stallion's spirit in a pretty package. Except...whatcha gonna do if you leave?"

"Go back home. I've been thinking about setting up a seamstress shop. I'm fast and I'm good. I think I could make a living at it."

"I got a sewing machine. If you get bored refereeing the two bulls, you can use it."

Mariah laughed outright as the kitchen door opened. "Thanks, Flo. If I stay, I'll consider it."

"*If* you stay?" Jud asked as he closed the door and came into the kitchen. "I told you. There's no discussion. You're staying."

This stubborn, angry man was not the cowboy who'd ridden over the snow with her, who'd made a special batch of chili one night so her mother could have a break, who'd kissed her so passionately yet touched her so tenderly. "I don't take orders. From anyone," she told him.

"Maybe you'd better learn how," he warned, his eyes narrowed, her duffel bag held in his right hand.

"Don't get all macho with me, Judson Thatcher Whitmore. You might order around the hands that work for you, you might do the opposite of what your father wants to spite him, but you will *not* tell me what to do." Mariah thought she heard Flo mutter, "Go get'em, girl," but she wasn't quite sure. The look in Jud's eyes should have made her run for the hills, but she sat perfectly still, her hand on her belly, and waited.

As he opened his mouth to speak, his gaze went to her hand protectively soothing her child and he snapped his lips shut. Motioning toward the living room with the duffel bag, he said curtly, "Follow me upstairs. I'll show you your room."

"Is that an invitation?" she asked calmly, again trying to make her point.

"Blood and thunder, Mariah! If you're going to fight me every minute—"

"I'm not fighting," she cut in. "I'm the mother of your child, Jud, not some piece of baggage you can toss somewhere until you decide what to do with me."

He looked as if he wanted to toss her over his shoulder and... Yep, she was sure that was a glint of desire in his eyes. But they'd need more than that to be parents.

All of a sudden, Jud looked more tired than angry. "Mariah..." He sighed. "I think it's best if you go upstairs and rest. Don't you?"

Out of the corner of her eye, Mariah saw Flo turn back to the counter to hide her smile. Her mother would like Flo and vice versa.

Seeing Jud had at least given an inch, she stood. "Resting sounds good."

Looking relieved, he started through the living room and was halfway across before he thought to wait for her. When he stopped, she was right behind him. He gave her a long probing examination with searching blue eyes. When she didn't say anything, he started forward again and up the steps.

Everything in the Whitmore house was utilitarian, from the scarred oak table in the dining room she'd only glimpsed beyond the kitchen, to the sofa and comfortable-looking chair and recliner in the living room. As she followed Jud up the stairs, she smelled lemon polish on the wood banister and rails. He took her past a closed door, rounded the stair-rail and strode past another. He stopped at the third. The fourth door at the end of the hall stood open. She couldn't see in and wondered if the room was his.

He nodded to the open door. "That's mine. Dad sleeps downstairs since his heart attack. We made the office into his bedroom."

"So it'll just be you and me up here?" Her mouth suddenly went dry at the thought.

"Unless you want to invite Flo and Mack to stay up here, too. But they kind of like the digs Mack built them. Feel you need some protection?"

Jud seemed to be much too big and wide and male at the moment. She could smell the scent of hard work, sun, and earth, all attracting rather than repelling her. "The house is big for you and your father. I just wondered."

Looking past her to the other rooms, he said, "My grandfather built the house for my grandmother. But the only survivor of the family was my father. The way I hear it, he and my mother intended to fill this place with kids. But it never happened. My father blames me."

The admission came from deep within Jud. Mariah suspected she should tread carefully. "How could he blame you?"

For a moment she didn't think he was going to answer. Then as if he'd been waiting to say the words for a long time, they burst loose. "My mother had trouble with my birth and was never the same after. A year later she died of influenza."

It was an absolutely ridiculous inclination, but Mariah felt Jud needed a huge hug more than he needed to be in charge or win an argument with his father. She also knew he wouldn't accept it from her right now. Nevertheless, she reached out and clasped his arm. "I'm sorry."

Their gazes met, connected and held. "Your mama told me your dad was killed riding a bull. How old were you?"

Mariah had seen her mother and J.T.—Jud, she reminded herself—talking now and then. They'd gotten along well. "I was ten."

"You knew your father."

She remembered a man with more smiles and hugs than responsibility, but she knew he'd loved her and her mother. "Yes, I did."

"I was too young to remember my mother."

Realizing she was still holding his arm, she released it and impulsively touched her fingertips to his chest. "No, you weren't. In here, some part of you remembers her rocking you and feeding you and loving you."

Covering her hand with his, he murmured, "You're only twenty-one and you think you know everything."

"I don't have to be older to know what matters."

"And that is?"

"When people love us, the love doesn't vanish when they're gone."

His fingers curled around hers and the heat between them became a flame of need that licked at her, making her wonder if she did need protection from her own desire, her own feelings for this man who was more of a stranger than she'd ever expected.

The firmness of his grip told her they weren't going to diminish the tension between them with mere words. When Jud bent his head, she told herself she could survive his kiss. It wouldn't make her want or need more than she already did. But she didn't get the chance to test her theory.

Because he didn't kiss her. He dropped her hand and backed away as if she was a new kind of devil he didn't care to know.

He pushed the door to the room open and swung her duffel bag onto the bed. "Supper's at five. Someone will call you if you fall asleep." Going over to the far side of the room, he flipped open the air-conditioning vent in the wall.

Mariah was less mindful of the dark pine dresser, bed and washstand than of the man who looked at her with fatigue and strain cutting deep lines around his eyes. The past few months had changed him so. "Jud, I didn't come here to cause trouble."

"There's always trouble when a man acts recklessly without considering the consequences." His bootheels came down hard on the floor as he made a wide circle around her on his way to the door. "I know you don't want someone telling you what to do, Mariah. But if you think about it long and hard, you'll know staying here, at least until the baby's born, will be best for everyone."

Then he closed the door behind him before she could refuse or argue.

Judson Thatcher Whitmore had a thing or two to learn about communicating with a woman. She didn't tolerate closed doors any better than she tolerated stubborn males. Right now she was too tired to do anything about it. But after she'd rested, he'd find out he couldn't close a door and expect her to stay behind it.

The horse Jud had brought into the pen needed working. But, damn, the heat wasn't as bad as his lack of concentration. This afternoon, he didn't think he could tell a good-minded horse from a bad-minded one, let alone have patience to work a green colt. Seeing that Mack and one of the other hands had everything under control, he went through the barn to the back where he'd moved his office.

Ignoring the computer and the stack of paperwork that had piled up again, he went to the phone, plopped his hat on the desk and dialed a number he'd long ago committed to memory. He'd thought about calling Luke, but Christopher seemed to have his head on straighter where women were concerned. Especially since Jenny's accident. Especially since they'd renewed their vows and left for a second honeymoon. Come to think of it, they might not even be home yet.

Since Jud had dialed Christopher's private line, his cousin and friend picked up himself. "Langston here."

"When did you get back?"

"Saturday night. I wish we could have stayed longer. But we had to return to the real world sometime. How's Uncle Thatcher?"

"As ornery as ever. This keeping my mouth shut so he doesn't get upset could drive me to pull out the whiskey."

Christopher chuckled. "And I'm sure he's not keeping his thoughts to himself."

"Never."

"Then what's going on?"

After a pause, Jud said, "Something else has come up."

"What?"

"Uh, remember I told you I did something really stupid while I was on that ranch in Montana?"

"Y…es," Christopher drawled.

"Well, she showed up here today. Pregnant." The silence that followed didn't give Jud a clue as to what his cousin was thinking.

Finally Christopher asked, "What are you going to do?"

"I don't know. For now, she's going to stay here. Unless she gets it in her head not to. She's a handful."

"What did Uncle Thatcher say?"

"He wants me to get married!"

"What do you want?"

"I never got the chance to find out, did I? I had to come back here."

"Seems to me you knew what you wanted the night you took her to bed," Christopher said matter-of-factly.

The slam came from nowhere. "Whose side are you on?"

"We've never pulled punches, Cousin. You don't sleep around. This woman—"

"She's only twenty-one," Jud cut in.

"This woman," Christopher repeated, "apparently got to you. Is there more than sex involved?"

"Jeez, you get personal."

"*You* called *me*. Did you just want to vent? Or do you want advice?"

Between dealing with Mariah *and* his father, Jud figured a little advice couldn't hurt. "Go ahead."

"She's pregnant with your child. That's a powerful connection. Don't do anything you'll regret until you're sure of what you want."

"Are you saying I shouldn't consider marrying her?"

"No."

"Are you saying I should?"

"No."

"Dammit, Christopher..."

"Do you really want my opinion?"

Jud raked his hand through his hair. He'd lived his life using his own judgment, depending on his gut. And his cousin knew that. "No, I don't want it. I've got to figure this out myself. She might be using this pregnancy to get more than support for the baby."

"Do you think she wants money?"

"I don't know what she wants. But one thing I've learned over the years is that women have ulterior motives."

"Not all women."

"You've got a good one."

"I know." After a pause, Christopher added, "Jenny was twenty-one when I married her."

"So you're saying age doesn't matter?"

"No. It does. If Jenny had been on her own when I met her, even a year out of college, we might not have fallen into the pattern we did. We might have had the marriage we have now from the beginning."

"Mariah's not as...demure as Jenny was."

"And that means?"

"She's not afraid to speak her mind."

"But you like that about her."

"Sometimes I do...sometimes I don't."

"You can't have it both ways," Christopher warned. "You also can't be married and act as if you're single. You can't be single and expect to have what's possible when you're married.''

"You're making this whole thing as clear as mud."

"That's the way it is, Jud."

"I've got to get back to work." When in doubt, work.

"Sure you do. Call me if you want to hash anything out.''

After Jud said goodbye, he shook his head. Maybe he *should* have called Luke. Luke had steered clear of commitment since he lost his wife. Since that day, he'd seemed to believe life should be lived to its fullest and that required many women, not just one.

You can't be single and expect to have what's possible when you're married.

Deep down, Jud knew Christopher was right.

He blew out a breath. But what did he know about marriage? Flo and Mack's was the only decent one he'd seen close up. His father's engagement had been a disaster. And as far as relationships between parents and kids...

All he and his dad had ever done was fight.

If he had a son, he wanted more than that. And if he had a marriage—

He swore, thumped his hat on his head and set out for the pen. Working green colts had to be easier than figuring out his life.

When Mariah awakened, it took her a minute to orient herself to her surroundings. Night had fallen, and upon opening her eyes, she'd thought she was sleeping in the bedroom she shared with her mother. She soon remembered the bed under her now was double, not single, the furniture sturdier and matching, the spread beneath her store-bought, not handmade. And the afghan thrown over her…

As she switched on the bedside lamp, she realized the room was much cooler now than when she'd fallen asleep. And someone had made sure she didn't get chilled.

Flo? Jud?

Her stomach grumbled, telling her it was long past supper. She'd get a shower, then go find something to eat.

She'd packed light, but she wasn't about to go downstairs in only a nightgown. Instead she took a pale pink overshirt and knit pants from her duffel. She'd made the set herself last summer and brought it along because the elastic at the waist would stretch with her waistline. As she came out of her room, she glanced at Jud's door. It was closed, and she didn't know if he was inside or not. Tiptoeing, she went into the bathroom and closed the door.

A half hour later, she felt like a new woman. Well, almost. She'd remembered a brush, but she'd packed so fast she'd forgotten a dryer. Although she'd towel-dried her hair the best she could, it was still basically wet.

Her feet bare, she tucked her clothes on the straight-backed caned chair in her room, then went downstairs. The clock on the mantel above the brick fireplace struck midnight as she reached the dark living room. But a yellow glow from the kitchen spilled through the doorway. Remembering Jud's father's bedroom was downstairs, she wondered if he was still up.

Instead of Thatcher Whitmore, Mariah found the kitchen light over the small trestle table shining on Jud's black hair as he turned the page of a newspaper. "You're awake," he said, startling her because he didn't turn around.

Apparently she hadn't been as quiet as she thought. "I didn't mean to keep you up."

Sliding his chair to the side, he propped his arm on the table. "You didn't. This is the only time there's silence. I take advantage of it."

His shirt was open down the front, the shirttails hanging out over his jeans. His chest was tanned, though not quite as dark as his arms. Black hair tumbled across it, thicker down the center. She remembered running her fingers through it, the feel of his hot, taut skin. Her heart started racing, and she combed her fingers through her wet hair to bring her back to reality. "I thought somebody would get me up for supper."

"Flo said to let you sleep. She left you a plate in the fridge."

Turning away from his probing appraisal, she opened the refrigerator and found a plate piled high. She slid it out and transferred it to the microwave. "Someone covered me."

"Dad had hiked up the air-conditioning. I didn't want you catching a chill on top of everything else."

When her gaze found his, she was sure he'd watched her sleep. Because she was a problem he didn't know how to solve? Or because he cared? "Thank you. But I can take care of myself. *And* my baby if it comes to that."

His jaw took an uncompromising tilt. "It won't. Do you honestly think I'd let my child go without?"

"I don't know, Jud. I'm beginning to wonder if I know you at all. You're not the same man who helped me check cattle, who joked, who made love to me in the barn." Her voice went low and huskier at the memory.

But anger flared in Jud's eyes. "Don't try to seduce me with those words you like to read in books. It won't work."

"I'm not trying to seduce you," she protested. Back in Montana she'd confided to him how much she liked to read. He'd teased her about a romance he'd seen sticking from her pocket one day.

"Oh, no?" he returned. "Is that why you're down here with your hair wet, your feet bare, and that outfit fitting you like a glove?"

Indignation stuck in her throat. "I didn't even know you were down here!"

"Didn't hear me moving around upstairs, did you?"

"I didn't listen. My world doesn't revolve around you, Judson Thatcher Whitmore." She laid her hand on her stomach. "It revolves around the baby. I felt dusty so I took a shower. I was hungry so I came down to eat. Your whereabouts had nothing to do with it." Her voice had risen with each sentence and when she finished, the microwave beeped, adding emphasis.

Still, he didn't seem fazed. Scraping his chair legs on the linoleum, he stood and crossed to the counter where she was. "Excuse me," he said, reaching behind her to a plastic holder that held a cake with chocolate frosting.

His bare chest, wavy black hair, and muscled strength were right in front of her nose. She was so tempted to wrap her arms around his neck, raise up on her toes... Now she *was* thinking about seducing him. Because he was being so...so...male?

Not a good reason.

Besides, she didn't know the first thing about seducing a man, and she'd better remember the fact.

Quickly stepping aside, she took her plate from the microwave and slid off the plastic wrap. A puff of steam broke loose, burning her fingers. The plate spun on the edge of the counter as she tried to contain a yelp.

Jud was there pushing the dish to the side of the sink, then catching her hand. "You're old enough to know better," he growled as he ran the cold water and shoved her fingers under it.

He was standing behind her, surrounding her really, which made it hard for her to catch her breath, let alone protest. The cold water did nothing to appease the fast-rising temperature in the kitchen as his hips brushed her bottom and his chest stayed plastered against her shoulder. She could feel every hard plane of him, every muscle, his belt against her side.

Not daring to move, she just stood there waiting until her fingers went numb and his scent became the air she breathed.

Finally he let go of her wrist and shut off the spigot. "Let me see," he said gruffly.

Leaning away from him, she grabbed a towel from the oven door. "I'm fine."

"Let me see," he said again with that restrained tone that told her she'd better not argue.

She dried her fingers, then held them up in front of her. "No blisters."

His mouth tight, he ran his thumb along her index finger, then across the next one. He was so gentle that she wanted to cry and blamed it on hormones. After an interminably long couple of seconds, or minutes, or hours—she wasn't sure which because she was simply relishing his callused touch—he said, "There's some salve in the bathroom. I'll get it."

As he moved away, she took a lung-filling breath and told herself coming here was the best thing to do for their baby. But at the moment she felt too muddled to believe it.

The face that looked back at Jud from the bathroom mirror was tight and drawn and filled with a tension that wasn't going to find release anytime soon if he had anything to say about it. Just thinking about Mariah...

He grimaced at himself in the mirror, then shook his head to clear it. Yes, he'd covered her. After Flo had told him to let Mariah sleep, he'd just wanted to check on her. He'd checked, all right. And watched her breasts rise and fall as she'd slept, felt the aching to smooth his hand over her cheek, comb his fingers through her hair.

Listing every reason why Mariah could be bad news, he'd left her room, trying to only think about the baby growing in her womb. He'd almost managed to forget about all of it for a few hours till she'd come sashaying into the kitchen, all shampooed innocence and tempting witchery. Her outfit hadn't been *that* tight, but it clung at all the right places—her slightly fuller breasts, her curvier hips.

All he had to do was stay out of her way till he

figured everything out. *So get the dang salve, give it to her and get out of the kitchen.*

After he had his cake. Mariah wasn't going to chase him away from Flo's chocolate cake. If he couldn't satisfy one appetite, he might as well satisfy another.

Flipping open the cabinet, he grabbed the tube of salve and shut the mirrored door, thankful his father had updated the downstairs bathroom with a shower and a new sink long before he'd needed it.

The convenience of the bathroom quickly got pushed aside as Jud saw Mariah savoring her supper. She'd just put a forkful of potatoes into her mouth.

He laid the tube on the table. "There you go."

After a quick look at him, she took the medicine, opened the lid and applied it to her fingers, which were still red.

"Take it up with you and put it on again in the morning."

Defiant lights sparked in her eyes, but she didn't say anything until after she'd finished a few more forkfuls and he'd opened the cake holder, cut himself a slice of cake and slipped it onto a plate.

"Do you really want me staying here, Jud? If you don't, I can find a place somewhere."

"At my expense, of course," he muttered, thinking she probably had an apartment in mind, not a room in a boardinghouse.

"I can stay nearby and take in sewing or get a job typing and filing or something. I'm perfectly capable of taking care of myself. Or...I can go home. I won't stay here if you're going to resent every minute of it.''

He didn't like ultimatums and wished he could believe all she was concerned about was the baby's welfare. But he'd had too much experience with women who'd dated him or slept with him because he was Thatcher Whitmore's heir rather than because their motives were pure. In fact, he'd *never* tangled with a woman whose motives were pure.

''Are you making this my decision?'' he asked.

''As much as keeping the baby is mine.''

Pain as sharp as an arrow lanced him, and anger covered it. ''Is that a threat? You'll keep this baby only if I provide you with everything you need? Or want?'' he added, determined to find that motive he was sure she was hiding.

Half of her plate still untouched, she stood as regally as a queen. ''I have never...*ever*...thought about anything but keeping this child. And you know what I need *and* want? A father for him or her who knows how to love and teach and guide. If you can't do those things or you don't want to try, then I don't belong here. And neither does my baby.''

Before he had a moment to form a thought, she'd left the kitchen and gone upstairs. He heard the sound of her bedroom door closing firmly, and he realized cynicism was a tough partner to live with.

Yet, he'd never had another.

Chapter Three

Pacing the kitchen, his slice of chocolate cake still sitting on the counter, Jud swore, hoping some of the tension in his chest would ease. He didn't *want* to want Mariah. He didn't want the tight feeling around his heart every time she protectively settled her hand on her stomach or mentioned the baby.

His baby.

Their baby.

The full reality of that fact was finally sinking in.

Her words echoed in his head. *I have never…ever thought about anything but keeping this child.*

Could he believe that? Could he believe her reasons were as pure as she wanted him to think? Or had seeing his picture and the write-up on the Star Four showed her a way to make her own life secure, to grab a life she might never find on her own?

He sincerely doubted she'd pack up her bags and leave. Yet, Mariah could be as unpredictable as a yearling. If she did go, he'd pay the price in more than money. Because she could use their child as a bargaining chip whenever she liked. At least if she stayed here, he'd have a say in everything that concerned his son or daughter.

A son.

A daughter.

His.

Nothing had ever been his. Even now, though he was virtually managing everything about the Star Four, it still belonged to his father. His year away had shown him he needed to be his own man; he needed to become more than Thatcher Whitmore's son. But his father's heart attack had made that damn hard to do.

If Mariah stayed, he'd have the chance to become more than a son. He'd be a father.

He had to convince her to stay.

Glancing at her dinner plate and the food that had grown cold, he knew *he* had to make the next move.

Mariah liked sweets, especially chocolate. She'd kept a stash of chocolate bars and, on cold Montana afternoons, she'd bring him one along with a thermos of coffee whether he was riding a fence line or working in the barn.

He'd always wanted more than the chocolate and, like a fool that February night, he'd forgotten she was twenty-one and too young to know better as they'd kissed then gone entirely too far. Too far for him to turn back. Too far for him to forget. He hated the way she made him need. He'd just have to push those needs aside and keep his mind on this baby.

After he pulled a glass from the cupboard, he filled it with milk and grabbed the dish with the chocolate cake and a fork to go with it. Taking the steps two at a time, he told himself to settle down so Mariah didn't get wind of just how much he wanted her to stay. With that in mind, he slowed his steps.

Standing outside her door, he didn't hear any movement within. He rapped and waited. When she came to the door, she was wearing a nightgown, but had wrapped the afghan from the foot of the bed around her like a shawl to cover herself. His good intentions fled and he felt as if he'd bitten the dust. Although the cover reached from her shoulders to her elbows, it didn't hide the deep V neckline of the pink striped cotton gown. Nor did it hang farther than her knees. Mariah's legs were long, curvy and slender and he remembered the feel of them entwined with his....

Quickly he cut off the memory and cooled his desire. Lifting the dish and the glass he said, "You didn't finish your dinner. I thought you might still be hungry."

"Room service, J.T.? Now *that* I didn't expect."

She wasn't going to make this easy. He should have known he wouldn't find her curled in a ball with tears on her cheeks. Not Mariah. "I told you my name's Jud. Are you still hungry or not?"

She didn't respond for a moment, and he could see she had a dilemma. If she took the plate and glass from him, she'd have to let go of the cover. So she wouldn't let go, something he wished for and dreaded at the same time, he said, "Why don't I put it on the dresser? Then if you want it, it'll be there."

With a wary glance, she stepped inside and let him pass by her. But she left the door wide open.

Her duffel bag sat on the floor beside a straight-backed chair. She'd left a book open on the caned seat. Picking it up, he read the spine. *Egypt and the Pyramids*. "A little light reading?"

"More like feeding a dream. I've always wanted to see them."

Her answer put him on guard again. She wanted to travel. She wanted a better life. "If you're planning on having this baby, I guess you'll have to postpone the idea."

"Dreams don't have time limits, J...um...Jud. Sometimes a dream you have to wait for is better than one that seems to happen overnight."

"Maybe a little planning and biding time doesn't hurt either."

She studied him, then finally asked, "What do you think I want?"

"More than you had. Money. A name that could give you respectability and a new life."

"I've always had respectability."

"Did you? Then why did you lay down with a drifter?"

Her cheeks went crimson and she didn't answer him. She just pulled the cover tighter around herself which only made it shorter and gave him a better view of her legs under her gown.

He blew out a breath. "Look, Mariah, we both made a mistake. I was older and should have known better. But I let some fool itch get the better of me. Now we have to muck out the mess. You said it's my decision whether you stay or go. I want you to stay...at least till the baby's born. I can make sure you take care of yourself. I can make sure I have a say in the start this child gets in life."

Embarrassed, Mariah had to gather her thoughts before she could answer. *Why did you lay down with a drifter?* How many times had she asked herself that same question? She'd given herself to him because she'd fallen in love with him. But now she had no illusions about what he felt for her. Not when he thought she wanted his money, possibly the Star Four. And as far as what he'd felt for her when they'd made love...he'd been scratching an itch. End of that story.

"What happens *after* the baby's born?" she asked.

"I don't think either of us is ready to answer that. We'll take it as it comes." His gaze kept passing over her as if he wasn't trying to look at any one place too long. But wherever his eyes focused, she felt heat and wished she didn't.

In Montana, there'd been no awkwardness between them. Now they seemed to be different people. Strangers...yet never strangers. To break the silence, she said, "I'll stay. Until the baby's born."

He gave a short nod, then another long look that sent prickles up her spine. "I've got to turn in. Flo usually has breakfast on the table around six. But you sleep as long as you want."

Once she heard everyone moving around the house, she'd be up with the rest of them. His kindness made her feel as if the old J.T. was back. How she wished he'd smile. How she wished he'd realize she came here because she cared about him and the child she carried.

Holding the cover around her with one hand, she gestured toward the milk and cake on the dresser. "Thank you for that. I'll enjoy it."

Silver flashed in his blue eyes. "I thought you might." Then he moved toward the door.

The play of his muscles under his shirt as he moved tempted her to look, to touch, to invite him to stay. But she knew better now; she'd learned her lesson well. She wouldn't be giving him any more pleasure for pleasure's sake. Because she wanted so much more.

Not looking back, he walked down the hall to his

door. She heard it open and shut. Then she closed hers.

Loving Judson Whitmore hurt, but she didn't think she could stop her feelings any more than she could stop the sun from rising.

The sun was bright and much higher in the sky than Mariah expected when she stepped out of bed. Checking her watch, she saw it was midmorning. Her trip from Montana must have taken more out of her than she thought. She couldn't believe she'd slept through the morning goings-on.

Hastily she dressed, ran her brush through her hair and went downstairs. Flo insisted on feeding her breakfast, and she wondered if Jud had given the order. After a last sip of juice, she went outside, and seeing activity in one of the corrals, she headed for it, determined to find something to occupy herself.

Jud's father was standing at the gate, watching a hand work a gray on a longe line. He tipped his hat to her. "Mornin', Mariah. Get a good night's sleep?"

She smiled. "I must have. The day's almost half gone."

He nodded to the man in the corral. "That's Mack. Our top hand and one of the trainers."

"And he's Flo's husband?"

"Yep."

"Think he'd let me help him?" she asked.

"Whoa, there. You're pregnant, girl. Don't you get it in your head we're gonna let you cut cows."

There was amusement in Thatcher's tone and a twinkle in his eyes, a slightly lighter blue than his son's. "Mr. Whitmore, I can't sit around with my feet up until I have this baby. That's not who I am."

"Cut the Mister, Mariah. It's Thatcher. I'm soon gonna be your pop-in-law. And I think Jud's gonna give you a fight if you go anywhere near one of the pens."

"But I can halterbreak yearlings..."

"I have a better idea. I heard Jud swearin' at the computer again. He hates doin' the book work. Why don't you go inside and tell him you want to help with that?"

She made a face. "I can understand why he hates it."

Thatcher gave a chuckle. "Start with the computer. Maybe he'll let you gentle the colts and fillies when he sees how strong you are."

When she raised her gaze to Thatcher's, she realized he'd given her a compliment, but meant it as fact not some idle flattery. "Mr...." At his raised brows, she quickly gave in to his request. "Thatcher, I told Jud I would stay until the baby's born. That's as far as it goes."

The elder Whitmore lodged his boot on the second rung of the gate. "I heard you two in the kitchen last night. Not on purpose, and I couldn't make out everything. But there's more between you than a baby. Give Jud some room, Mariah. Like I said before, he'll come around.''

Already she guessed there was no point arguing with Thatcher Whitmore. "Right now, I just want him to let me do something to keep busy.''

Thatcher tipped his head toward the barn. "The computer's in there—in the back next to the tack room.''

Hurrying inside, Mariah headed for the cubicle that looked freshly built. She could smell new lumber. The door stood open, and Jud sat in front of a computer at a built-in desk. He looked up, his gaze meeting hers.

"Hi,'' she said softly. "I'm looking for something to do. Your dad thought I might be able to help you with the book work.''

"He did.''

It wasn't a question but she knew he wanted an explanation. "First, I offered to help with the horses...''

"You're pregnant, Mariah. Get it out of your head.''

Protective males. Two of them in the same house! She suspected Jud was a lot more like his father than he wanted to admit. "Yes, I'm pregnant. Not sick or disabled. If I'm careful...''

"The first careful thing you're going to do is go into town and see a doctor. I checked around and found one who came highly recommended. I made you an appointment for this coming Monday at ten.''

"I saw a doctor before I came. I have vitamins. He said to just use my good sense.''

"Yes, well, you need someone here. I'll take you in case there's anything I need to know.''

"You're *not* going to be my keeper.''

"I wouldn't dream of it. But I'm the father of your child, and I'll make sure you take care of him.''

"Or her,'' she flared, wondering if he just wanted an heir.

"Or her,'' he agreed with a slip of a smile.

Her flash of temper subsided. "What about some help with the paperwork?''

"So you can know all my business?''

"Your *business* didn't cross my mind. I need something to do to fill my time, to feel I'm earning my keep. But if you're so thrilled to handle it yourself, fine. I'll use Flo's sewing machine and make some maternity clothes. Maybe I'll even take in sewing. Then you won't have to worry about giving me pocket money.'' Without waiting for his response, she turned away and headed for the door. Some way, she'd keep her independence. Some way, she'd show Jud she was more than an inconvenience he had to put up with until their baby was born.

The afternoon passed quickly as Mariah got acquainted with Flo's sewing machine. The housekeeper had shown her to a spare room in the small ranch house where a stack of material, remnants and threads tumbled over each other on her worktable. Mariah's own machine was much older, and Flo's was a joy to operate.

The housekeeper left Mariah alone while she went to start dinner at the main house, insisting she didn't need help. But as dinnertime approached, Mariah felt she should lend a hand. She found Flo peeling potatoes, a pudding of some sort cooling on the counter.

"What can I do?" she asked.

"Well, I guess we could give Thatcher a treat tonight and let him have a biscuit so he doesn't complain how tasteless dessert is." Flo waved at the cooling dishes. "Sugar substitute. Low fat." She sighed. "If Mack and I didn't eat with him and Jud, I know he'd cheat on his diet. I think he does anyway. I make treats for Jud that disappear too fast."

Mariah crossed to the flour canister. "Do you do anything special with the biscuits? Mama taught me how to make them before I learned to write."

Flo nodded. "I would of guessed as much. Use the skim milk and skimp on the shortening. I don't use lard anymore." Finishing the last potato, she washed her hands and said, "I'm gonna get the clothes from the line. Rolling pin and everything else you need is in that cupboard to your right."

After Flo left the kitchen, Mariah spotted a small radio by the microwave. She switched it on and country twang filled the air. Even though Thatcher was on a diet, she'd bet Mack and Jud could eat a batch of biscuits in no time flat. She'd better double her recipe.

The dough mixed, she was about to flour the pastry cloth when the hair on her neck prickled. She stopped humming along with the music and glanced over her shoulder. Jud stood inside the door, watching her, his eyes shadowed by the brim of his hat. As he approached her, the simple task of transferring flour from the canister to the cloth became complicated, and she closed her fingers around it.

"Where's Flo?" he asked.

Her heart pounded harder. "Getting the wash... from the line."

Jud's boots were dusty, and so were his jeans that fit him the way every man's jeans should fit. She remembered unsnapping them.... As he stopped a foot from her, the smell of horses and hard work wound around her, pleasing her like everything else about him. He was the picture of a cowboy—hard and tough—but in Montana she'd gotten a glimpse of the kindness and gentleness underneath. Yet right now it was the slant of his lips that drew her gaze, and the sudden tension in the air knocked everything else out of her head. The heat from the oven had made the kitchen stifling in the past few moments.

"I thought you'd be resting." His voice was gruff.

"I slept late this morning."

"Still..."

"Jud, I know what I need."

"Maybe. Maybe not."

"You have to trust me to take care of myself and the baby."

Swiping his hat from his head, he set it on the table. "I don't trust anyone, Mariah, especially women."

His words hit her like a blow. His attitude went much deeper than suspicions about her motives. "You were so different when we met. What is it about this place that makes you so...cynical?"

"You didn't know me, Mariah. You met the man I was pretending to be. A cowboy on vacation from reality."

"No. I don't believe that."

When he stepped closer, she supposed he meant to intimidate her but his body so near to hers certainly didn't change her mind. If anything, it revived the memory of every word, every kiss, every touch.

"Just make your biscuits, Mariah."

"Or what?" she challenged when he didn't step away and the silver flickers in his eyes told her biscuits were the last thing on his mind, too.

"Damn you," he growled as he brought her against him and lowered his head.

If she hadn't realized it before, she did now. She'd wanted this since February, dreamed of kissing him again, being held in his arms. His lips on hers were possessive, held no coaxing quality, only demand.

Flour sifted through her fingers as she brought her hands up his shirt and clasped his shoulders.

Pure instinct led her rather than good sense as his tongue speared through her lips. She let him take what he pleased, hoping he'd remember another time, another place. His tongue stroked feverishly against hers, making the curling in her womb wind tighter and tighter...

"Well, isn't this a sight! Does my heart good," Thatcher exclaimed.

Jud tore away, swearing, then swiped his hand over his lips as if he was trying to erase the kiss and the passion they'd kindled. "Stay out of this, Dad."

"Out of it? Hell, I want to announce it. Why don't we have a big barbecue on the Fourth of July?"

"There's nothing to announce," Jud snapped.

"From the looks of your shirt, more than cookin's goin' on in here." Amusement and satisfaction fairly vibrated in Thatcher's voice.

Jud snatched his hat and didn't bother brushing the streaks of flour from his shirt. Waving the brim at his father, he said, "No barbecue. And no announcement. I mean it. Don't fight me on this."

The two men's gazes locked and neither seemed to want to be the first to turn away.

Finally Thatcher asked, "Or you'll leave again?" He grunted. "I'm beginning to think you comin' back here was a big mistake."

"It's a shame we're both just realizing that now,"

Jud said as he walked out the door. The screen door swatted shut behind him.

The expression on Thatcher's face when Jud turned his back and left urged her to go to him. He didn't seem to see her until she clasped his arm. "You know what I think?" she asked softly.

The older man's eyes glistened a bit. "What's that?"

"He's overwhelmed by taking all this on. And he's still worried about you."

"I'm fine. And I think you're seein' things that aren't there. He wants his own place, his own time, his own life. Maybe I've been wrong forcin' the Star Four on him."

"Jud's a strong man. He wouldn't be here unless some part of him wanted to be."

Patting her hand, he smiled. "You might be young, but you're smart."

She thought about daring a proud cowboy a few moments ago. and the kiss that had resulted. "Sometimes I'm not so sure." When she noticed the flour on the floor, she said, "I've got a mess to clean up. Any idea where Flo keeps the dustpan and brush?"

"I'll take care of the flour. You just roll out those biscuits. I'm lookin' forward to havin' one while everyone's watchin', and sneakin' another when they're not."

"Thatcher..."

"Just jokin', Mariah. Just jokin'!"

But she suspected he wasn't. If Jud was worried about his father, he might have good reason. But he'd probably never confide in her like his father had.

I don't trust anyone, Mariah, especially women.

Sometime soon she was going to find out why.

Flo, Thatcher, and Mack carried the conversation around the table as Jud avoided Mariah's gaze. He'd stirred up a hornet's nest earlier and if he looked at her, he'd stir it up all over again. He never should have gotten that close to her. Angry at himself for giving in to desire he didn't want to feel, he broke apart a biscuit—his third—and reached for the margarine.

"Dang good, aren't they?" Thatcher asked, nudging his son's elbow.

"They're fine," Jud answered.

"If you've got a hankerin' for bakin'," Thatcher said to Mariah, "You might want to enter somethin' in the bake-off at the fairgrounds on Saturday. First prize this year is a hefty gift certificate from the mall."

"I've got the rules for it," Flo added. "I'm thinking about entering myself. There's three categories— pies, cakes and breads."

Mariah glanced at Jud. "Sounds like fun. If I won that gift certificate, I could make some things for the baby."

Jud buttered his biscuit. "You can buy anything

you want for the baby. You can charge it to my account.''

''Women need to nest, Jud. Store-bought's not the same as making something with your own hands,'' Flo explained.

''You oughtta open a checking account for her, Son. That way—''

''I'll take care of this, Dad.'' Mariah would more likely abuse a checking account than bills he went over once a month.

''Excuse me. I…uh…need something in the kitchen.'' Mariah pushed back her chair and left the table.

Jud had heard the slight quiver in her voice, and he knew something was wrong. He didn't need the glare from his father to make him get to his feet and go after her.

When he found her, she was standing at the door looking out, her arms crossed over each other as if she were cold. Walking up behind her, he stood close enough to smell her shampoo. ''Thinking about leaving?''

Without turning around she answered, ''No. Thinking about how I'm going to stay. I called Mama and told her I was, but…''

He believed in getting to the root of her upset, not fencing with words. ''What's the problem, Mariah?'' If she thought he was going to give her carte blanche with his or the ranch's funds, she could think again.

His father had traveled that road with his fiancée. Jud wouldn't let himself be as easily manipulated.

"I'm not used to having my business discussed around the supper table!"

Her dismay sounded real. "There are no secrets on the Star Four."

"And no privacy, either?"

Taking Mariah's shoulder, he nudged her around. Could she really be embarrassed about others looking after her?

"Privacy's hard to find when Dad's around. After a while, it gets to feel as if even your thoughts aren't sacred."

Studying him, she saw beyond his words. "That's a big reason why you left, isn't it? To make sure your thoughts were your own."

Mariah's perception always surprised him. He never expected her to be old enough to have it. "It's one of the reasons."

She sighed. "I've only shared my thoughts with my mother all these years. No one else knew our business or cared. We lived with Mr. Hopkins, but he was a loner, and Mom and I stuck together. This is just going to take some getting used to."

When he looked into her eyes, he believed she'd been embarrassed. But there was something else, too, and it probably had to do with money as he'd first guessed. "And?" he prompted.

She bit the side of her lower lip, and he wanted to

kiss her much more thoroughly than he had before supper. Damn, why did she rile his hormones and make him need like a stallion around a mare in heat? He dropped his hand from her shoulder.

Lifting her chin, she answered him. "I don't want to feel like a kept woman."

"You're the mother of my child. I'll take care of anything you need."

"You still don't get it and you should. You don't want your father running your life, and I don't want you running mine. I need to feel I'm earning my keep."

"We've been through this—"

"No. *You* have. Without listening to me. I need to feel I'm an independent woman, not a baby machine or someone who needs to be taken care of. Let me help with the Star Four somehow. You know I'm good with horses."

"Mariah…"

"Or," she rushed on, "let me keep vet records or worming schedules. I don't have to go near the ranch's books."

He shook his head. "It's all on the computer. If I give you access to one file, you've got access to all of it."

"And just what am I going to do with it? Maybe I don't know exactly what this place is worth, but if I'm around for the next few months, I'll certainly figure it out."

She had a point there. Mariah was snap-quick at adding up and figuring out. It wouldn't take her long. And in the meantime, the stack of paperwork on his desk would grow into a mountain. He understood about needing independence. He just wished he could be sure that was her only motive. But he supposed he'd find out quicker if he gave her some rope.

Tucking his thumb into his belt loop, he thought about her offer one more time. "All right. Tomorrow after breakfast I'll give you a lesson or two on the computer and we'll see how you do. But for now I think we'd better get back to the table or they'll *all* be out here eavesdropping."

Mariah smiled then, a full wide smile he hadn't seen since February. And he felt as if he'd just stepped into a deep mud bog that could swallow him up before he had the chance to even try to pull himself out.

Breathing deeply, Mariah walked toward Jud's office, her heart tripping faster. She liked the smell of horses and leather, liked the welcome nicker of the mares as she passed them. Jud's capitulation in letting her help him might make her feel part of all this...as if she had a place in his life.

His office door stood open and she found him at his desk, his head bent as he filled in an order form. Hearing her footsteps, he looked up.

"Sorry I wasn't up when you were," she apologized. "I'll have to get an alarm."

"I can only spare a few minutes—enough to get you started. One of the owners will be here anytime now."

"I'm a fast learner. What do I do first?"

He bit back a grin. "How about turning it on?" Then he motioned toward the buttons for the computer and the monitor.

When he stood, she slipped into the chair he'd vacated. With him standing behind her, she was aware of the fresh scent of soap and his own male scent. Their kiss in the kitchen seemed as close as his body heat. Leaning away from the temptation of both, she flicked on the switches and waited for him to direct her.

He told her which buttons to push, and she wrote his directions on a small notepad for future reference.

Taking a stack of receipts from one of the shelves, he said, "We'll start with something easy. March, April and May's supplies. It's past the middle of June and I still haven't entered these."

Mariah paid attention as he showed her what to do. She could see why Jud hated doing it; the work was time-consuming.

A shout came from the front of the barn. "Shelby's here."

Jud called back. "Be out in a minute. Take her to the arena and get her started."

Quickly he showed Mariah how to save data she entered on the hard drive as well as on a backup disk. Then he frowned and looked over his shoulder.

"Go on," she said. "I think I've got it. If I have any questions, I'll save what I have and work on the rest this afternoon."

After he studied her for moment, he nodded. "Later, I'll show you how to print it out and you can check what you've done. I'll be tied up till lunch at least." Then he took his hat from the rack on the wall and left her there.

Mariah worked steadily, double-checking the figures she entered, carefully putting an *X* on each receipt to note its entry. But then she came to a supply store receipt that looked like a carbon. The numbers were impossible to read, the total indecipherable. She thought about just setting it aside, but curiosity and a need to stretch her legs urged her to save the work she'd done and find Jud.

Outside, white pipe fencing stretched in every direction. Mariah followed the path to the indoor arena. It was metal and housed some stalls, with aircraft hangar doors on either end that were open now to allow for ventilation.

Thatcher stood on the sidelines, watching his son and a beautiful blonde on a black horse. Even from here, Mariah could tell the woman wore makeup and had styled her curly hair around the wooden barrette at her temple. She wore gray jeans and a matching gray shirt with native American designs in red and black across the shoulders. A little dressy for working, Mariah thought.

"Back him up. Slow him down," Jud called to her. "You've got to give him time to think. He's smart. Let him do his work."

"Come to watch?" Thatcher asked with a sideways glance.

The paper in her hand forgotten for the moment, Mariah nodded, keeping her eyes on the cow, the horse, Jud and the blonde.

"Cutters are special," Thatcher explained. "They have to think. We don't just teach 'em patterns. We train them to respond to the cow. Riders can't use the reins, but they can use their knee pressure to help guide the horse. Understand?"

"The rider has to be in tune with his horse."

"That's it. And usually Shelby is. Leastways, she is when her sights are set on winning a run rather than on Jud."

Mariah watched as Shelby and her horse worked the cow while Jud called instructions and two other hands on horseback held back about fifteen head. Finally Shelby pulled up her horse, left the cow, and stopped near Jud. When she dismounted, she did so very close to him, and he didn't step away.

With their heads together, their voices low, Mariah couldn't hear their words. "Who is she?" Mariah asked.

"Shelby Vance."

"Not her name. What is she to Jud?"

Swiping his hand across his brow, Thatcher cupped Mariah's elbow and pulled her into the midday breeze. "Jud trains her horses."

"And?"

Thatcher chuckled, shook his head, and rolled his eyes. "A woman's sixth sense is nothing to sneeze at, I always say. They've gone out now and then. Shelby likes to two-step."

From the way the woman was possessively clutching Jud's arm and smiling up at him, Mariah would bet the blonde preferred slow dances even more. "Does she live near-by?"

"Not within yelling distance but close enough."

"And she'd like to be a lot closer," Mariah murmured.

Thatcher patted her shoulder. "Now don't you worry none. *You're* carrying Jud's baby."

"That doesn't count for much if he wants someone else."

"Honey, are you gonna run without a fight?"

She looked at Shelby's head so close to Jud's, she remembered his kiss, and she started toward him before she changed her mind.

Chapter Four

The closer Mariah got to Shelby Vance, the more she felt like fighting. Only she wasn't sure how. As she took the blonde's measure, she realized the woman was old enough to know her way around men, young enough to make every flutter of her lashes innocent-looking. How could she fight when her own man-woman skills were so lacking?

Clutching the receipt as if it were a ticket into Jud's world, she approached him with a confidence she didn't feel.

Jud's brows arched under the brim of his hat. "Is there a problem?"

She handed him the receipt, then hoping she was wrong about Shelby, extended her hand to her. "Mariah Roswell."

Shelby eyed her as if she had no business interrupting a training session. Yet, Mariah knew there was more going on than training. The blonde ignored her hand and said simply, "Shelby Vance."

Mariah watched Jud look up from the receipt into Shelby's questioning brown gaze. It seemed she wanted an explanation for the interruption. He must have decided to give it because he offered, "Mariah's staying at the Star Four for a while and helping me catch up on the paperwork that backed up."

Shelby waited for more but when she didn't get it, she put one hand on her hip and asked, "She's living here?"

Impatiently Jud responded, "She's a friend of the family." He returned the receipt to Mariah. "You'll have to call the feed store for the figures. You might want to make sure there aren't any more like this before you do."

It was a simple solution that Mariah would have thought of herself—if she had given it some thought. Right now she was more upset that Jud considered her "a friend of the family" rather than the mother of his child. Obviously he didn't want Shelby to know she was pregnant with his baby.

The dismissive glance he gave her told her she'd already taken up too much of his time…with Shelby. Quick tears burned in her eyes and she blinked them away. "Sorry to bother you. But I couldn't finish up March without checking on this." Then she turned away, determined not to stay where she wasn't wanted.

Feeling Jud and Shelby's gazes on her, she walked back to Thatcher. "I just made a fool of myself," she mumbled to him on her way to the door.

He clasped her elbow. "No, you didn't. You threw your hat in the ring. But it wouldn't hurt to let him think about it while we get some lunch. He won't quit out here till he gets accomplished what his mind's set on."

"Shelby skips lunch, too?"

Thatcher looked chagrined. "She brings sandwiches and a thermos so they can eat and work. She knows Jud."

Mariah had thought she'd known J.T., but now she wasn't so sure. Maybe J.T. and Jud really *were* two different men.

As Jud lifted his hat and ran his hand through his hair, he watched Mariah talking to his father and felt a twinge of...he wasn't sure what. They got along, that was obvious.

He'd seen the hurt in Mariah's eyes when he'd told Shelby she was a family friend. But what was he supposed to say? He'd been a damn fool and wasn't sure what was going to happen next? Mariah was so young. What if she decided motherhood was too much of a burden? What if she ran out and left their child with him? What if she didn't? What if she just wanted his name and his money?

Questions that went round and round in his head in the dead of night...along with the need that sometimes had him waking in a sweat. Mariah was a complication that was making him forget his own name.

Shelby crossed to a bench and picked up a bottle of water. "Are you still going to escort me to Daddy's party?"

Otis Vance's spread was larger than the Star Four, but strictly a cattle operation. The shindig he and his wife planned every June was one of "the" social events in Tyler. Not that Jud cared, but Thatcher always claimed their appearance was good for business.

But this year... "I don't know, Shelby."

"Jud, you promised. It was bad enough you dropped out of sight for a year without telling me where you went, you at least owe me a fun time at Daddy's party to make up for it."

She was half teasing, half pouting and today both irritated him. Shelby had always wanted him to show more interest in her than in her horses. Sometimes he'd complied to entertain them both. But Shelby knew it was only a good time and that "long-term" wasn't in his vocabulary.

Yet leaving like he had, when he'd returned he *had* promised her he'd be her escort for her father's party. "All right. You know I keep my word. If you want an escort, you've got one."

Her smile turned all honey as she came toward him, her water bottle forgotten on the bench. Bracing her hand on his chest, she said, "You know I'll make sure you have a good time. And maybe after some mingling and dancing, you and I can find a quiet place to spend a few hours."

Although he'd like to forget about Mariah, Shelby's offer didn't even tempt him a little. Her fingers resting on his shirt caused no reaction inside him, didn't make him ache with the need simply being around Mariah stirred up.

Backing away from Shelby, he said, "Let's just start with the party and see what develops from there. Meantime, we've got some work to do. Hey, Randy. Let's get fresh cows. Blazer's not stopping with the cow and I want to figure out why."

He understood horses much better than he understood women.

Tyler, Texas, was large enough to have shopping, conveniences, and a medical center that had saved Thatcher's life, as well as being small enough to foster community spirit. That spirit was evident at the craft fair and baked goods contest at the fairgrounds on Saturday evening. Mariah walked along a table that bore baked goods from the three different categories, wondering if her endeavors would pass muster as the judges tasted them. The huge red canopy set up for the contest's entries kept the late-day sun from her, but the air was hot and humid and she was glad she'd sewn herself a sundress.

She'd stayed out of Jud's way the past couple of days and he'd stayed out of hers. After he'd shown her how to print out the figures she'd entered in the computer, after he'd checked her first batch of work for accuracy, he'd left her on her own. For the most part at mealtime, he kept silent, and she had no clue as to what he was thinking.

When Flo had again encouraged Mariah to use her sewing machine, she'd found scraps of material in Flo's pile of fabric leftovers to fashion the patchwork sundress yesterday. Flo had lent her a pair of plain leather sandals that she'd insisted caused her a blister. Mariah knew the housekeeper was being kind, and she'd soon have to face buying a few things with her savings. It was one reason why she'd entered the contest. That gift certificate could make her self-sufficient a little longer.

Groups of onlookers were gathering around the tables. Suddenly Mariah's senses went on alert and she glanced over her shoulder. Jud stood at one of the support poles, watching her. She'd ridden into town with Flo and Mack. She supposed Jud had driven Thatcher.

When her gaze met his, he started toward her.

Suddenly Mariah felt self-conscious in her home-made dress and borrowed sandals. The way his eyes moved over her from one bare shoulder to the other shortened her breaths. She'd pulled her hair back into a low ponytail and tied it with a red ribbon, but she could feel stray tendrils wisping along her cheeks. Wishing she felt tidier, she brushed them away from her face.

"All set for the judging?" he asked.

"As set as I'm going to be. They have at least thirty entries in each category."

"I had a slice of that second loaf of cinnamon bread you made this morning. It was good."

"Don't sound so surprised," she teased.

"Lots of things about you surprise me, Mariah. Especially the way you look today. I'm used to seeing you in jeans."

She felt her cheeks color. "A girl likes to feel a skirt around her legs once in a while."

His gaze drifted from her hem down her calves to the sandals. "You sure fit a lot into that duffel."

Before she could tell him differently, Thatcher came up beside his son. "You two oughtta take a walk over to the craft stands before they shut down. I saw a pretty shawl the color of Mariah's eyes. Might be nice to wear to the Vances' party next Saturday."

"Shelby's having a party?" Mariah asked, sure the woman wouldn't want her around.

"It's her daddy's party. He throws one every year." Thatcher looked at his son. "Are you gonna show Mariah that we Texans know how to have a good time?"

She could have sworn Jud's cheeks flushed with more than the heat as his jaw took on a stiff tilt and he answered, "I'm taking Shelby."

Mariah's heart felt like a dead weight.

"You're what?" Thatcher bellowed. Then he lowered his voice. "This pretty young lady here's carrying your baby and you want to go sashayin' around with that spoiled—"

Clasping Thatcher's arm, Mariah stopped his outburst. "It's all right. I'm not the party type. You can't expect Jud to change his life just because I dropped into it."

"The hell I can't!"

Jud had that frustrated expression on his face he often got when he and Thatcher disagreed. "Mariah understands. Just drop it, Dad, before your blood pressure goes sky-high."

"My blood pressure would be just fine if you'd get some sense."

"You mean if I do what you want me to do. I've been doing that since February and it's starting to feel a lot like blackmail. Mariah and I will handle our business ourselves. Stop meddling."

Mariah stood by, unsure of what to do as the two men glared at each other. When a voice came over the loudspeaker, she sighed in relief as Thatcher looked away and over at the judging stand.

"I'm getting a better view," he mumbled, then ambled toward the podium.

The tension between her and Jud was as thick as the humidity. "I don't want to come between you and your father."

"There's a lifetime between me and my father. Don't worry about it, Mariah. It's not your concern."

The idea of him taking Shelby to a party, and Thatcher's protective meddling that might be hindering more than helping, made her flare up. "Just what *is* my concern? Not you. Not Thatcher. Not the Star Four. What am I doing here if none of it's my concern?"

"You're preparing to have a baby."

Lowering her voice, she said, "Not just any baby, Jud. *Your* baby. I can't forget that, but you sure seem to be trying to."

As Jud opened his mouth, to protest she supposed, the microphone squeaked, then settled. A red-faced, balding man adjusted the height of the mike. "We have our winners."

Mariah waited, intensely aware of Jud beside her.

The man at the podium announced, "We'll begin with the third place winners. For her cinnamon swirl bread, a twenty-five dollar gift certificate goes to Mariah Roswell."

Mariah heard Thatcher cheer, and Flo gave her a thumbs-up sign from across the tent. The third place awards in cakes and pies were also announced to more rounds of applause, then the second place winners. To her delight, Flo won first place and a two hundred dollar certificate for none other than her chocolate cake.

"I could have bet on that one," Jud said. Then he nudged up the brim of his hat. "I told you your bread was good."

His satisfied tone made her smile. "I should have let you taste test all my entries. Maybe then I could have won first place, too."

She saw the flecks of desire in his eyes that told her he might be thinking about tasting something else...like her lips. Then she remembered he was taking Shelby Vance to her party. "I'd better go get my gift certificate."

As she turned away, he caught her elbow. "Would you like to get some supper? There's everything from fried chicken to chili."

Her pride told her she should refuse, but her heart echoed her desire to spend time with him. "Fried chicken sounds good. I'll be right back."

She knew the smile on her face was much too wide for just winning third place. But she didn't care. She was going to have supper with Jud.

They strolled side by side, not touching, rarely talking, but Mariah felt Jud's gaze on her often. She snuck peeks at him. His jeans looked new—a concession to going into town rather than working horses. His blue, western-cut shirt was crisp, his boots were black, not the brown ones he wore on a daily basis.

But the hat was the same, as were the chiseled line of his jaw and his deep blue eyes.

Walking from stand to stand, Mariah tried to keep her attention on the crafters, the pottery, the silver and turquoise jewelry. But Jud's body heat, the slow drawl of his voice as he made a comment or asked a question kept her focus diverted. Until she saw the stand of shawls. Until she remembered Thatcher's hint to Jud that he buy one for her. She hurried on. He already thought she wanted a lot more than shawls or baubles. And she did. But what she wanted had nothing to do with money.

Finally they stopped walking. Jud turned to her and said, "Why don't we buy the chicken dinners and get out of this crowd? I know a pretty spot at the edge of town where we can eat."

"That sounds nice." A picnic with Jud. Some time alone. That might be just what they needed.

As they walked toward the food stand, Mariah saw Jud frown, his gaze on a spot behind her. When she looked over her shoulder, she spied Thatcher at a french fry stand pouring salt on the cup of fries he'd bought.

"Should we stop him?" she asked.

Jud shook his head. "It won't do any good. If we take those from him, he'll find something else just as bad."

"How serious is his condition?"

"The doctors wanted to treat him with medication

and by putting him on a strict diet first. But he thinks he's invincible! If he has another heart attack…'' Jud let out a breath. "I don't know what to do with him."

"He might say the same about you."

"He might. But he doesn't understand that if I'm going to live my life on the Star Four, I have to do it my way. He can't put me in charge then second-guess me."

"You're his son, Jud. I can't say I know everything he's feeling, but since I found out I'm going to be a mother, I feel fiercely protective. Like I'd do anything to protect this child and keep him or her safe. Being a parent must change the way you look at the world."

When Jud's gaze passed over her face and came to rest on her lips, she thought she saw a tenderness there she'd never seen before. The aromas of chili and chicken and fries wafted around her on a slight breeze as he leaned toward her. The noise and the smells and the sounds around her faded with the touch of his finger sliding across her lower lip.

"It's hard to believe you're going to be a mother," he murmured.

She didn't want to change the moment, to lose the wonder in his eyes or the gentleness in his voice. But they both had to face reality. "I *am* going to be a mother. It's hard for me to get used to the idea, too."

When he leaned away, she knew they'd lost that moment of connection and she wasn't sure why. Along with fighting his father's domination, Jud was fighting his feelings for her. Why? What had made him so cynical? Maybe if she learned that, she'd know how to get closer to him.

At the stand he bought chicken dinners, biscuits, drinks and pie for dessert. Then they found Flo, Mack and Thatcher to tell them they were leaving.

The last light of the day was slipping from the edge of the horizon as Jud made a right turn then pulled off the side of the road and parked. He grabbed a blanket from the back of the truck. "We just have to climb that hill and go through the stand of pines."

When he came around, he opened her door for her as the shadows played over the trees. The hill they climbed wasn't steep, but he cupped her elbow firmly to give her support. His callused palm on her skin sent shivers dancing through her.

Jud guided her through a small grove of pines to a clearing. Then he deposited the bag of food by a tree and spread the wool blanket. "This beats all that noise and people at the fairgrounds." Lowering himself to the ground, he took off his hat and set it next to him.

Mariah sat on the blanket beside him, her legs curled under her skirt. "You don't like crowds?"

With a wry grin, he said, "I live in a crowd. Ever notice how many people are always around? Trainers, hands, owners, not to mention my dad. I'll get enough of people and noise at the Summer Classic in mid-July."

"What's that?"

"One of the biggest events for cutters. It lasts two weeks." He handed her a box of chicken, then opened his.

"Do you compete?"

"Sure do."

For the next few minutes they concentrated on their food, sipping long swigs of their drinks. Jud got a far-off look in his eyes as he ate a biscuit and looked into the distance.

"What are you thinking about?" she asked softly.

His shoulder brushed hers as he shifted toward her. "Last year at this time."

"Where were you?"

"On a spread in Wyoming."

There was something she'd wondered about Jud. As soon as she'd arrived, she'd called her mother to tell her she was fine and settled for a while. But already she was missing her more than she could imagine. She'd gotten a letter from her yesterday, but it wasn't the same as talking in person. Hadn't Jud missed his home? "Did you miss being here?"

"Some. But I needed to be there more."

"If Thatcher hadn't had a heart attack, would you have ever come home?"

"I don't know."

Jud had accepted his responsibilities but he wasn't sure how they fit or *if* they fit. And now she'd saddled him with another that would last a lifetime.

Dusk faded into night as they ate their pie with plastic forks, the quiet moments between them filled with more peace than she'd felt since she'd arrived. She treasured each one as she and Jud sat there alone together, not wanting the time to end. Eventually Jud gathered up their debris and set it off the blanket.

His voice was low and deep when he said, "We'd better get going."

Even on Sundays he got up early, and she knew they should leave...but neither of them jumped right up. When she turned toward him, he turned toward her, their shoulders still touching. Night shadows played over the thatch of black hair dipping over his forehead and wrapped around them until she believed they were the only two people in the world.

She didn't move; she didn't blink. Because she knew if she did, the spell would be broken and he'd put distance between them again.

But distance didn't seem to be on his mind as his lips brushed hers...slowly...as if he didn't want the moment to end, either. He grazed her mouth with his again as his large hand caressed her bare shoulder. The kiss turned serious. His lips were firm on hers, insistent, and she knew they were toppling on the brink of should-they or shouldn't-they. It was her choice.

She didn't think as she brought her arms around his neck, she simply felt and there was nothing simple about it. He laid her down on the blanket and slid his tongue into her mouth. She accepted it; she accepted him—the long length of his body against hers, the desire he was still holding in check, the need he didn't want to acknowledge.

When he slipped the strap of her sundress over her shoulder, she ran her hands over his arms, exploring him once again. His shirt was an unwelcome barrier, and she wished she could brush it aside as easily as he had her strap. Slipping one hand to the nape of his neck, she stroked him there.

He moved against her and she felt his desire. As he passed his hand over her breast, he realized she wore no bra and he deepened their kiss. Mariah's head swam with the intoxicating sensations, the smell and feel and heat of him. The kiss seemed to go on forever, whirling her in a passionate world she'd only experienced once before.

Before he was called away.

Before she'd found out she was pregnant.

Before she'd become a responsibility he was determined to honor.

Did she want him like this? She'd gotten caught up in the moment the first time with him and look what had happened. Did he really want her? Was she more than a convenience so he could satisfy his needs? How did Shelby fit in?

Sliding her hands to his shoulders, she pushed slightly. Jud broke the kiss and lifted his head.

So many questions clicked through her mind but

one stood out. "Are you still taking Shelby to the party?"

His scowl was apparent even in the darkness. After he took a few breaths, he pushed himself up. "I told you I was."

"But this…us…tonight…"

"Just because we spent the evening together and ended up kissing doesn't give you rights over me. Dammit, Mariah. You turn up in the barn and expect the world!"

"No. You *think* I want the world. You think I want money or a stake in the ranch. What I want is respect." Sitting up, she straightened her shoulder strap, then got to her feet. "Ended up kissing, you say. Well, understand this, cowboy. Don't think you're going to kiss me like that again while you're seeing someone else."

She didn't wait for him but used the brightening light of the moon to guide her to the pines.

"Mariah! Mariah, wait."

Neither his call nor the curse he let out stopped her. But he caught up with her before she went down the hill. While he gripped the blanket under his arm and the remains of supper in a bag in one hand, he firmly grasped her elbow with his other. Seeing her safely in the truck, he slammed the door.

The tension vibrated through the air blowing in the windows the whole way back to the Star Four. When he stopped at the walk to the house, she hopped out and hurried inside, straight up to her room.

The front door of the house closed, and Jud gunned the truck.

He *wasn't* seeing another woman.

Not really.

This thing with Shelby…he was just taking her to a party because he'd given his word.

Growing up, Jud had learned giving his word was as serious as a promise. If you went back on it once, you'd do it again. Except this time…

Damn. Mariah was making him one foot from crazy. As soon as he'd seen her today with her bare shoulders, her hair pulled back, his heart had raced. She got under his skin just as she had back in winter, the first time he'd seen her. Half the time he felt guilty he'd gotten her pregnant, the other half he wanted to lay her down in the hay again. But he still wasn't sure of her motives.

With Shelby he knew exactly where he stood. She wanted a good time. She wanted to be queen of Tyler. Between her parents' wealth and the Star Four's reputation, a marriage between them would make the state sit up and take notice. But he'd never led Shelby on. He'd never pretended something he didn't feel. He'd told her time and time again marriage wasn't in the cards.

Parking the truck in the shed, he switched off the

ignition. Why had Mariah traveled here unless she wanted something? Once she knew about the Star Four, she could have sent him a letter about the pregnancy. She could have phoned! But she'd come with a bag in hand instead. Had she known him well enough to determine his sense of honor wouldn't let him turn her away?

He remembered his father's fiancée, the way she'd run up bills on his dad's credit cards, the way she'd walked around the place as if it was already hers, the way she'd betrayed his dad by sleeping with the help. He thought about Shelby's maneuvering to spend as much time with him as she could, her pretty pouts, her seductive smiles. Ever since he was old enough to ask a girl out, he'd known daddies as well as daughters would welcome him because of the Whitmore name.

And now he'd bet his favorite pair of boots that Mariah wanted that name as much as she wanted respect. Well, what she wanted and what she'd get were two different things.

Because no one would force him into a marriage he didn't want...not even a green-eyed temptress whose smile could make the sunshine seem dim.

Since Mariah tossed and turned all night, she was up before sunrise and down at breakfast before Flo even popped toast in the toaster. Jud wasn't in sight. She'd heard his bootheels on the floor earlier.

Thatcher's gaze gave her a thorough going-over. "He skipped breakfast. That boy never skips breakfast. And you look as pale as the moon. You two have a row?"

She didn't want to discuss last night with Thatcher. Like Jud, she'd rather keep her private life private. But he was waiting for an answer, and she knew he wouldn't let it go. "You might say that."

Flo asked, "Eggs or pancakes?"

Mariah wasn't the least bit hungry. "Just toast this morning."

The housekeeper put a plate of fresh toast on the table. "I'm gonna collect laundry. You make sure he just eats his cereal and fruit. Nothing else."

Mariah nodded and Flo went into the living room and up the stairs.

"Everybody thinks they're my keeper," Thatcher grumbled.

Jud and his father were so much alike, yet they'd both deny it. "I guess they don't think you keep yourself very well."

With a harumph, he poured skim milk on his cereal and made a face. "You fought about Shelby."

"Thatcher..."

"I know. I know. You want to tell me to keep my nose out of it. If I do that, you two are gonna waste a lot of time. Life's too short for that. I think we need to do something to shake Jud up a little."

The way she saw it, maybe Jud's life had been

shaken up too much lately. "I don't want to make him resent me, Thatcher, or wish I was gone."

"That's right. You need to do the opposite. How would you like to get all gussied up and go to that party with me on Saturday night?"

"I couldn't do that!"

"Why not? Can't I escort my daughter-in-law-to-be to a party?"

She had to smile. Thatcher really was incorrigible. And it might be good for her to see how Jud and Shelby acted together, what exactly *was* between them. Yet there might be another problem. "How fancy is this party?"

"Pretty fancy. You need to go to town for something to wear? I'll gladly pay the tab."

"No, I can't let you do that. But I did win that gift certificate… I can make myself a dress."

"A party dress? You can do that?"

She laughed. "I can try."

Thatcher's face broke into a wide smile. "So you'll go?"

Jud had never seen her all gussied up, as Thatcher put it. If she fixed her hair, bought a tube of lipstick, made a dress that would knock his boots off… Why not? Just seeing the expression on his face would be worth the effort of making ten dresses.

"Yes, I'll go." Then maybe Jud would take count of her as a woman as well as the mother of his child.

Chapter Five

When someone knocked on Mariah's door Monday morning, she'd just snapped the catch on her jeans. She could barely close them now so she let her top hang out instead of tucking it in. She'd slept late again, but not so late that she couldn't take a shower before her doctor's appointment. Opening the door, she was surprised to see Jud standing there hatless, his jeans already dusty from a few hours of work.

"I'll be ready in fifteen minutes to take you to town," he said.

After what had happened Saturday night, she'd thought he might let her drive herself. He'd hardly said two words to her since then. "I don't need you to chauffeur me. I wouldn't want to take you away from a training session." She would have added "with Shelby" but decided not to push her luck.

"Mack, Randy, and Ted can handle everything just fine till I get back. I'll meet you downstairs."

And before she could blink, he headed for his room.

The ride into Tyler was silent. When they'd kept company in Montana and had quiet between them, they'd been comfortable together. At least she had been. But now, this tension made her edgy. Yet whenever she attempted conversation, he gave her a one-word answer. So at least for now she stopped trying.

When they arrived at the doctor's office, the receptionist smiled and gave Mariah papers to fill out. She sat next to Jud and completed a history. He must have been watching because when she came to the billing section, he asked, "Do you have medical insurance?" When she shook her head, he took the clipboard from her and filled in his name and address as the party to bill.

Obviously, Judson Whitmore took his responsibilities seriously. She just wished he'd feel more than responsibility.

When the nurse called her name, she stood. Glancing over her shoulder, she saw Jud had gone back to reading his magazine.

The obstetrician was kind, and Mariah was glad she was a woman. She didn't comment on Mariah's unmarried status or make any judgements. As her doctor had in Montana, Dr. Thomas examined her, told her what vitamins were best, gave her a diet for good nutrition for her and the baby, and asked her to return in a month. When Mariah asked if she could ride, the doctor smiled and said as long as she didn't enter any jumping contests and was careful.

After she returned to the waiting room, Jud met her at the receptionist's window and paid the bill. As they walked back to the truck, Jud looked at her and asked, "How did it go?"

"Fine. I like her. She let me listen to the baby's heartbeat. She had this special instrument that was attached to an amplifier."

"You actually heard it?"

At the excitement in his voice, tears came to Mariah's eyes. She nodded and swallowed. "Dr. Thomas said everything looks perfectly okay. But she asked if I wanted a sonogram. I knew that would cost so I—"

"The cost isn't an issue. If she thinks you should have it, we'll go right back in there."

"No. I mean, I could have it next time if I want to see the baby. If *we* want to see the baby. You could come in with me."

"You wouldn't mind?"

"Of course not. You're the father."

Once inside the truck, as Jud switched on the ignition, she caught the slip of a smile on his face. He cared about the baby even if he didn't care about her. Taking advantage of the mellow moment, she informed him, "Dr. Thomas said I can ride as long as I'm careful."

Any trace of a smile disappeared as he pulled out of the parking lot. "No way."

"Jud, I've been riding since I was three. It's probably safer than traveling in a car."

"A car doesn't have a mind of its own. Forget it, Mariah. I mean it. Or I'll confine you to the house."

She tried to hold onto her temper, but it was a losing battle. "You'll confine me to the house? Get over yourself, Jud. You can make suggestions. You can't give me commands. If I choose *not* to ride, it's because I'm taking your fears into consideration. *Not* because you gave an order."

On that note, she folded her arms across her seat belt and looked straight ahead.

She'd actually heard the baby's heartbeat.

Jud swiped his wrist across his sweated brow. As he exited the arena, he adjusted the brim of his hat against the sun, thinking about his trip with Mariah to the doctor's yesterday morning. A sense of duty had prodded him to take her. Finding out she had no medical insurance, he'd been doubly glad he went so he could take care of the bill.

No medical insurance and a child on the way.

Another reason for her to turn up on his doorstep. He'd have to call his company and see about getting her insured.

As Jud made his way to the mares' barn, he heard activity in the round pen. His trainers were in the arena. The hands were checking fence and moving cattle.

Curiously heading toward the round, fenced-in area, he saw his father sitting in a lawn chair a few feet away cleaning tack. When he opened the six-foot-high gate into the pen, he stood stock-still. Mariah was talking to a colt, an old straw hat on her head that she must have found in the barn. She scratched the animal around his ears, then with slow but certain moves went around to his side and ran her hands over his back and under his belly. She kept talking as she gentled him.

"What in blue blazes are you doing in here?" he asked as he crossed to her, noticing her T-shirt had a V that drew his gaze there.

The colt skittered. She grabbed his halter and laid a hand on his neck. When he quieted, she gave him an encouraging pat. "Good boy."

"I'm helping," she said to Jud. "You don't want me to ride so I won't. But there's no reason I can't work with these fellas."

"Why can't you act like a pregnant woman and go take it easy?"

She blew her bangs from her forehead and looked as if she was counting to ten. "These are the nineties, Jud. Pregnant women work in the home and outside of it. They keep fit, exercise, and live their lives the same way they did *before* they were pregnant. Dr. Thomas said I should do my normal activities...what I always do. I love being outside, I love riding, I love working with horses. If I can only do two out of three, okay, but don't think I'm going to sit in the house and vegetate until I have this baby!''

Thatcher appeared in the pen. ''She's got a point. It isn't healthy sitting around all the time. The doctors told me that.''

''You're not pregnant,'' Jud snapped.

His father gave a hearty laugh. ''If men had babies, there'd be a lot fewer of them, I'm sure.''

Jud didn't appreciate his dad's homespun philosophy at the moment. His attention back on Mariah, her gentle hand on the colt's neck, he asked, ''What do you intend to do with him?''

Mariah shrugged. ''Just rub him and handle him, brush him. Get him used to me touching him. I won't spoil him.''

''Look at him,'' Thatcher said. ''Already she's got him quiet enough to take a blanket.''

Jud knew his father was right. Looking at Mariah's hopeful expression, remembering her smile as she'd spoken to the horse and taken her hands over him, watching the sun pick up the red highlights in her hair, and thinking she'd never looked prettier, he gave in.

''All right. You want to gentle the colts, go ahead.

But don't get any ideas about trying a saddle on them. Randy and Ted will handle that. Agreed?"

Mariah's smile lit up her face. "Agreed."

The urge to kiss her was so strong he knew he had to get out of the pen before thought became action. His dad followed him out.

Jud pushed the brim of his hat higher on his forehead. "Did she ask you about doing this?"

"Mariah's not the type of woman who asks permission when she wants to do something. I found her in there and thought I'd keep an eye out."

"I'll tell *everybody* to keep an eye on her. I don't want her taking any chances."

"She just wants to feel she's doing something worthwhile the same as the rest of us."

Jud glanced over at the rag and leather cleaner his father had been using. Since his heart attack, he'd had to cut back on many of his activities. Jud wondered if he was having a hard time feeling worthwhile. But it wasn't something he could ask. Unless Thatcher brought it up on his own, he wouldn't like his son asking those kinds of questions. Running the Star Four was still a touchy subject between them.

"I've got to call the vet about one of the mares," Jud said. "Tell Flo I won't be in for lunch. I'll get something when the sun's too hot to do anything else." He took off toward the barn but felt Thatcher's gaze on his back. And decided he didn't want to know what his father was thinking.

* * *

It was almost 9:00 p.m. when Jud came in from the arena. Working in the evenings was easier and healthier than trying to work at the hottest time of the day. He'd get a shower, then grab leftovers Flo was sure to have set aside for him.

Wondering where he'd find Mariah, he climbed the stairs. He'd seen her drive off with Thatcher around three and return about an hour and a half later. Flo had said something about them going into town for supplies. He'd supposed she'd meant groceries. They'd probably saved her a trip. Carl, one of the hands, went into town to stock the bunkhouse kitchen every Saturday. But his cooking for the men was a lot different than what Flo made. Especially now with Thatcher on a special diet.

At the top of the stairs, Jud saw Mariah coming out of her room. She was wearing the same soft pink outfit she'd worn the first night. And her hair was wet again as if she'd just taken a shower. But it was her face and arms that snagged his attention. They were pinker than usual.

"Did you take off your hat while you were working in the sun?"

She gave a small shrug. "When I took a break. Then I forgot to put it back on. It just felt so good to be outside with the horses again."

He lifted her chin with his knuckle. "This Texas sun isn't kind. You should wear a long-sleeved shirt when you're out, too."

"I know. And I'll make sure I keep the hat on in the future."

"Does it hurt?"

She wrinkled her nose. "It just feels a little hot."

"Did you get ointment when you were in town?"

"I didn't notice this then."

Catching her elbow, he said, "C'mon. I have some in my room."

When she stopped just inside the doorway of his bedroom, he tried to see it through her eyes. The oak and black metal headboard was utilitarian, and the oak dresser with its black iron knobs and pulls was clear of debris except for an old china plate where he left his change and keys. A tall ceramic light stood to one side. Beside the bed, two nightstands held lamps made of horseshoes. The parchment shade bathed the room in a yellow glow as he turned one on. A pair of jeans, belt dangling, slid over a ladder-back chair, and dirty socks straggled on the floor by the bed.

She stared at the spartan forest green spread that covered the king-size bed. His gaze went to the bed, too. He remembered their time in the barn in Montana, touching her, holding her, losing himself in her. He'd never acted that impulsively in his life. But then he'd had no one to answer to but himself. He'd known he'd be leaving, that eventually he'd have to come back here. Had that one fling with Mariah been rebellion on his part against all the responsibility he knew he'd have to eventually take on?

That lapse of good judgement in the barn had left him with more responsibility.

Going to the chest, he opened the top drawer and took out a jar of cream. Despite all his doubts, feeling the attraction to Mariah so strongly he could taste it, he crossed the room and handed it to her, unable to resist teasing, "Need help?"

Her eyes grew wider but she tilted her head and gave him a sassy smile. "I can reach every place I need to reach."

Since only her face, neck, and arms needed attention, he was sure she could. But he'd definitely like to reach a few other spots as well as kiss them.

Kissing Mariah did something to him. It snatched the lid off his self-control and made him need like he'd never needed before. He remembered their last kiss, lying over her on the blanket, her words when she told him she wouldn't kiss him again while he was seeing another woman. Suddenly he wished he could break his promise to Shelby. Suddenly he wished he was taking Mariah to the party on Saturday night. But a man's word was his bond.

Still he bet if he drew Mariah toward him, she wouldn't resist a kiss. They might even end up on his bed. But no matter what his doubts were where she was concerned, she was the mother of his child and

he owed her respect. That's what she'd said she
wanted and that was one thing he could give her.

Her tongue crept out, licking her lower lip, and he
knew she was thinking about kissing and maybe
more. But he'd left his reckless streak in Montana.

He took a step back and so did she.

"I'm going to take a shower." His voice was
husky and he wished standing here with Mariah didn't
affect him any more than standing in the training
arena with Shelby. But there was no comparison.
"Are you turning in?"

"I'm going down for a glass of lemonade and then
I'll turn in," she said. "I wanted to read but I'll probably be asleep before I get very far. I'll see you in
the morning."

When she turned from his room, he had the strang-
est urge to call her back. But his horse sense prevailed
and he closed his door.

He wasn't in Montana now. He was managing the
Star Four, and he'd better not forget it.

The black patent high heels Mariah had found on
sale at the mall had at least three-inch heels. She'd
practiced walking in them this afternoon. She hadn't
worn heels like these since her high school gradua-
tion.

When she gazed into the full-length mirror on the
closet door in Flo's sewing room, she could hardly
recognize the woman who looked back. The black

taffeta dress was fancier than anything she'd ever worn. Her sunburn had faded into a light tan, and the dress sleeves hid the difference on her arms. Although she'd cut the V of the neck to follow the line of the T-shirt she'd worn, the point of the dress's neckline went a few inches deeper. She'd lined the bodice so she didn't need a bra. Her skirt was straight and short, but she'd added a flounce from the waist to mid-hip to hide her stomach which wasn't flat anymore.

Her creation was totally impractical. In another few weeks it probably wouldn't fit at all. But she'd managed to buy the material and zippers and such with her gift certificate. She'd only dug into her savings a little for the shoes, curling iron and hair dryer. Oh…and the lipstick and nail polish.

But now she felt ready to face Jud and Shelby. That's what mattered.

There was a soft rap on the door. "Thatcher's here," Flo announced with a smile that made her a co-conspirator. No one had told Jud she was accompanying his father to the party.

Mariah picked up the small taffeta purse she'd fashioned with its satin drawstrings. After making sure every curl of her upswept hairdo was in place, she took a deep breath and went to the living room.

When Thatcher saw her, he grinned. "Why, darlin', you could be on the cover of one of those glossy magazines!"

She laughed. "So could you."

Thatcher wore a dark brown western-cut suit, a beige shirt and a string tie. He offered her his arm. "Then we're gonna cause quite a ruckus when we walk in. Let's skedaddle."

The ride took about twenty minutes. The longer Thatcher drove, the more nervous Mariah became. Finally they turned onto a paved road bordered by fence and loblolly pines. It wound around a hill until it straightened again and led to a stately stone and brick mansion. That's the only word Mariah could think of for the huge house. Her heart pounded harder.

Thatcher pulled up to the pillared front entrance. A man in a black shirt and black jeans opened the door of the four-door truck and helped her out. Thatcher handed him the keys then took her arm and led her up the steps. At the top he paused a moment. When she glanced at him, his face was flushed and sweat stood on his brow.

"Are you all right?" she asked.

"I'm fine. Just a little indigestion."

"Did you sneak something you shouldn't have?"

"Maybe I did. Maybe I didn't."

Before she could pursue the conversation, half of the double stained glass door opened and a maid led them inside.

After Thatcher mopped his forehead with his handkerchief, he pushed it back into his pocket. "I'm just hot because of this dang getup. C'mon. Let's make our grand entrance, then I can dump the jacket."

When he offered her his arm again, Mariah placed her hand lightly in the crook of his elbow, needing the support. Jud had stayed clear of her since the night he'd given her the cream for her sunburn. She was sure she was the last person he'd expect to see now. On the way over, Thatcher had told her his son had already left for the party.

The room they stepped into was more ballroom size than living room size. There must have been fifty people mingling on the bare polished plank floor. A three-piece band was set up in one corner. A few couples danced to the tune. Pine sofas covered with cushions in native American prints sat along three sides, while large watercolor paintings of cowboys and horses decorated the walls along with wrought iron sconces.

"Vance moves out the rugs and some of the furniture so his guests can dance. Food's back there in the dining room and there's a couple more rooms off of that for sitting. C'mon. I'll show you."

Mariah didn't know what she expected when she got to the party. She wasn't even sure what she was supposed to do! But it didn't seem to matter because men and women kept coming up to Thatcher as they moved from room to room and eventually back to the ballroom. He introduced her as a friend of Jud's who was staying on the Star Four for a spell. Then somehow she got drawn into conversations about East Texas and horses. No one looked at her as if she didn't belong. When a maid came by with a tray of champagne, Mariah declined but Thatcher took a glass and a long sip.

As she gave him a scolding look, he leaned close to her ear and said, "Now don't spoil my fun. I'll only have one."

He seemed fine again in the house's air-conditioning without shedding his jacket. What could she say to him? He was a grown man who had to take his own health in his hands. But she'd watch him. More than one drink and *she* was driving home.

Suddenly she felt an awareness that made her heart trip. She hadn't seen Jud since she'd arrived, but she'd heard more guests were sitting and talking outside on the patio. When she glanced around the room now, she saw him standing by the band, watching her. She'd expected to see surprise on his face. But what she saw was an iciness that turned her blood cold. As he approached her, she couldn't help but think how handsome he looked in his starched white snap-button shirt, string tie, black jeans, and boots.

When he came up to them, he said to his father, "You didn't tell me you were bringing anyone."

"And you didn't ask. Couldn't let the little lady sit at home and mope while we were havin' fun, could I?"

Jud's gaze raked her up and down. "Doesn't look to me as if she has anything to mope about." He took her arm none too gently and said, "I'd like to have a word with you."

"Now, Son, I was just going to give her a turn around the dance floor. And you know once I start, she'll have a line waiting to keep it up. She's getting along with everyone real well."

The expression on Jud's face should have made Thatcher back off. Somehow she'd landed in the middle of a father-son duel which wasn't what she'd planned at all.

"Oh, I can see how well she's getting along and that's what I want to talk to her about." Jud's shoulders were as stiff as his voice as he pulled her toward the dining room.

Thatcher arched his brows, but Mariah shook her head and gave him a smile that told him she didn't want him to interfere.

Jud shepherded her through the dining room, past the table full of food, the bar with a bartender, and guests talking and drinking, down a hall to a closed door. Opening it, he tugged her inside a wood-paneled study with shelves of books, a desk and a leather sofa.

Pulling away, she asked, "What's your problem, Jud? You could have just asked me to come with you."

"And you would have come?"

"Of course! Why not?"

"Because you're having too much fun with my father.'' His tone was low and angry and she didn't know why.

Her own temper rolled into a boil. "What's the matter, cowboy? Aren't you having fun? Maybe you came with the wrong date!"

He stepped so close to her, she could smell his aftershave and see the tiny scar above his left brow. When he spoke, his words were as rough as his expression. "At least my date isn't wearing a dress with a neckline cut to her navel."

Automatically her gaze dropped to the V between her breasts which didn't even show any cleavage. "You're exaggerating."

"Not by much," he growled. "If you're trying to get my dad all riled up, forget it. His medication has given him a…slight problem."

Jud's implication was clear and she felt her cheeks flush. "What an awful thing to say, let alone think." She turned away from him and headed toward the door.

But before she could take a step, Jud caught her wrist. "You can't get to *me,* so you're trying to get to my father. I won't let you use him, Mariah. Maybe he bought you that fancy dress and introduced you to his friends tonight, maybe you've got him whispering into your ear, but he'll never marry you so don't think he'll be a backup if I don't pop the question."

Hurt, even more than anger, brought her hand up

before she was aware of it. She slapped Jud with as much strength as her trembling would allow.

He looked stunned, and then she didn't see anything else as he crushed her to him and sealed his lips to hers in a stinging kiss. All the gentleness she'd known in him was lost in the fire of desire. His lips branded her right before his tongue seared her. It was hot, erotic, so seductive she forgot their argument and remembered their passion.

She heard her purse fall to the floor as she dropped it to wrap her arms around his neck and lose herself in his need. It became her need. Roughly, he took from her as if he didn't want to, as if he was still fighting the way they got to each other. The more he demanded, the more she gave…freely. His breaths became harsher as he backed her to the sofa. He took her down with him, never breaking the kiss, never giving her the chance to tell him she wanted him as much as he wanted her.

And he did want her. She could tell from the hungry strokes of his tongue, the tension in his arms, his hand going to her zipper. He had it down and her dress off her shoulders so fast, she hardly had time to think about unbuttoning his shirt. But she wanted to touch his skin so badly that she pulled the cotton from his trousers, hoping to reach up underneath it.

By then, he'd laid her back on the sofa and she felt his arousal against her thigh. Jud had excited her the first time he'd looked at her. His body pressing onto hers led her beyond excitement to an aching she knew only he could satisfy. Once before, he'd made her feel every bit a woman. And now...

Breaking the kiss, he lowered his mouth to her breast and teased the tip. She moaned, the streaks of heat from her breast darting straight to her womb. His tongue wet her nipple, and her breaths broke in a gasp as she dug her fingers into his shoulders. His hand stroked up her thigh—

"Oh!" the female voice was a loud, clear interruption.

Jud's sharp words were as inelegant as the situation when he pushed himself upright and turned to Mariah, pulling her dress up to cover her breasts, shifting on the sofa to protect her from Shelby's gaze.

"Daddy told me he saw you come this way." Shelby stepped deeper into the room. "Looks like I should have knocked."

Though Mariah appreciated Jud's efforts to shield her, she was determined not to let her embarrassment show, especially not to Shelby. The woman's blond hair was curled in ringlets around her face. Her bright red dress was slim and sleek and short. She didn't look upset but self-satisfied, almost glad that she'd interrupted. Mariah itched to wipe the tilted smile from her face.

Sitting up, Mariah rearranged her sleeves and zipped up her zipper. "Or you should have stepped back out when you saw what was going on," she returned with a direct stare.

"Mariah…" Jud warned, his voice raspy.

They'd been a heartbeat away from making love, and he was as affected as she was. But she knew he'd never admit it. She knew he was going to act as if it had never happened.

"It's *my* house," Shelby informed Mariah with a lift of her chin.

"So it is," Mariah said as she stood and pushed down the flounce on her skirt. "And you want to give your attention to one guest in particular. Well, he's all warmed up for you."

At her words, Jud stood and looked as if he wanted to throttle her. She wasn't afraid of him. She knew no matter how angry he got, he'd never hurt her. He wasn't that kind of man. But his silent cowboy routine was making her crazy, and she intended to claim her territory before Shelby could give her another patronizing smile.

Mariah picked up her purse from the floor and went to the door. "But before you plan a romantic night for two, you might want to ask him if he wants a boy or a girl for his first child. Because come winter, he'll have one or the other."

Glad she'd practiced in the high heels, she hurried down the hall while the going was good.

She might have put up a confident front for Jud and Shelby, but she was shaken when she reentered the living room. Thatcher, with his jacket over his arm, rose from one of the sofas and came toward her. "What's wrong?"

"I just made a fool of myself again."

"Do you want to go back to the ranch?"

"I don't want to cut short your evening."

"I'd rather be sittin' on the porch counting stars. C'mon. Let's hit the road."

As Thatcher drove, he switched on the radio and left her to herself. He glanced over at her a few times but didn't ask any questions.

When they returned to the ranch, Mariah thanked him for asking her to go along and kissed him on the cheek. No matter what Jud thought of his father, the man had a good heart. She went to her room and undressed, her thoughts jumbled, her feelings unsettled. If she stayed, she was afraid she'd make everything worse between Thatcher and Jud. She was afraid Jud would resent her presence more and more. Maybe if she put some distance between them, they could both see more clearly.

After she crawled into bed, she went over everything in her head—the time in Montana with Jud, finding out she was pregnant, her trip here, her revelation to Shelby. Through all of it, she'd acted on instinct and impulse and maybe she'd been wrong. Lying there in the dark, she made a decision she thought would be best for everyone.

Whether she dozed or not, she wasn't sure. But

eventually she heard boots in the hall. Jud's boots. His steps slowed at her door.

"Mariah?" His voice was low, not loud enough to wake her if she'd been asleep.

But she didn't answer. She couldn't face him again tonight after what had happened in the study. And tomorrow?

Tomorrow she'd be gone.

"Where is she?" Jud demanded as he strode into the kitchen Sunday morning.

Thatcher kept reading the newspaper. "If you're talking about Mariah, she's probably still sleeping."

"No, she's not. Her room's empty and her duffel bag's gone."

At that Thatcher laid the paper on the table. "'Gone?' Where could she have gone? You don't think she went back home, do you?"

"I don't know, but I intend to find out. Somebody had to see her this morning. Unless she left last night."

His father shook his head. "I doubt that. She was quiet and kind of pale when I brought her home. What the hell did you do to her anyway to make her take off?"

Jud had been feeling guilty about his jealousy last night, his anger when he thought she was making a play for his dad. If the fire hadn't been so hot between them, that scene in the study never would have happened. "What did *I* do? You buying her that dress and taking her to the party was a stupid idea. Was it yours or hers?"

Thatcher frowned. "It was mine. You can't hide her away here like something you're ashamed of. And by the way, she made that dress herself. Used that gift certificate she won. Wouldn't take a red cent from me. She's not like most women we've known, boy. When are you gonna get that through your head?"

"You haven't known her long enough to know. She could just be a lot smarter. Innocence is a great act."

"Hogwash. Mariah is what she is."

"Your track record's lousier than mine, Dad. I have to make up my own mind about Mariah, but I have to find her first."

On his way out the door, Thatcher said to him, "Call me when you find her."

Jud gave a wave of his hand to say that he would, then went to question the hands. One of them had to know something.

Chapter Six

It only took Jud a few minutes to find out where Mariah had gone. He must have been in the mares' barn when she asked Mack to take her to town. At least she wasn't trying to cover her tracks. Then again, maybe she wanted him to go after her.

Damn! He didn't know what to believe about Mariah any more, but he was going to find out what she was up to.

Gunning his truck, he sped down the road heading toward a small motel on the outskirts of Tyler. She'd given Mack the address and told him that's where she wanted to go.

Why?

At first the desk clerk wouldn't tell Jud which room Mariah was in...said he had to call first. But when

Jud slipped him a twenty, the clerk had shrugged and revealed the number. That in itself proved the place wasn't secure enough for her. He climbed the outside stairway, thinking at least she'd had enough sense to take a room on the second floor.

When he found Room 233, he knocked and waited.

Mariah opened the door wearing her jeans with a blue T-shirt, and he thought she looked every bit as pretty as she had last night all dolled up. But his mind shouldn't be on that. Her cheeks flushed when her gaze met his.

"Can I come in?"

After she nodded, she went into the room, then stood there silently until he shut the door. He didn't like it when Mariah was quiet because he suspected trouble was brewing. Usually she said her piece without a second thought. Since she wasn't about to offer any explanations, he guessed he'd better start.

"Why did you leave?"

"Lots of reasons."

She could be the most exasperating woman. "Name one."

Tilting her head, she studied him. "I don't want to come between you and your dad. Whether either of you knows it or not, you need each other right now and I don't want to get in the way."

Her reason surprised him. Since she'd arrived, he thought she'd used the tension between Thatcher and himself to solidify her position. After all, she was proof of his foolishness while he'd been away. If nothing else, that would ingratiate her with his father who was always looking to point out his shortcomings.

"Dad and I would argue whether you're there or not."

"Maybe. But it's like I raised the level of competition between the two of you somehow. Thatcher thinks he has to stand up for me with you, and you think…" Her voice caught. "I'm not interested in your father, Jud. If I could choose another dad in this lifetime, I'd pick him. That's all."

He believed her on that one. As soon as the words had popped out of his mouth last night, he'd regretted them. But seeing her looking so beautiful, so tempting, with other men eyeing her as if they wanted to undress her, had pushed him beyond patience.

"And last night," she went on. "I can't believe I acted like that. I have never, *ever* in my life even come close to hitting anyone. I'm truly sorry. It's the biggest reason why I left. I don't want to turn into someone I don't know or like."

His guilt mounted. "Look, Mariah. Last night we were both at fault. I goaded you. I never should have said what I did. I'm sorry."

The astonishment on her face was so genuine, he felt even more like a horse's ass. He couldn't help stepping closer to her. "Come back to the ranch."

She shook her head. "I don't think it's a good idea.

You have your own life. I just barged into it. I don't have any rights where you're concerned, and you can see anyone you please. I can only do what's best for me and the baby.''

He couldn't believe the sinking feeling in his stomach. He didn't want to lose his child...that's what it was. "And it's best for you and the baby to stay in a two-bit motel?"

With a frown, she went and sat on the bed, looking up at him. "Of course not. I have enough money to stay here for a week and still have fare home. If I don't find a job in that time, I'll go back to Montana."

When he heard her determination, he respected it until he wondered if it was an act. Would she really leave Tyler? He couldn't take the chance on calling her bluff. Not if he wanted to be a father to his son or daughter.

Crossing to her, he sat beside her on the bed. "We've gotten off to a rocky start, but that doesn't mean we can't smooth it out. I want you at the ranch where I can see you getting big with my child. I want you to get plenty of rest and fresh air and eat right so you and the baby stay healthy."

Her shoulders squared. "I can take care of myself, Jud."

He couldn't help but smile. "Oh, I know you can." Laying his hand on her knee, he said, "But I want to help you do it. So do Dad and Flo and Mack. If I don't bring you back home, they might run *me* off the place.''

She finally smiled at his absurdity. ''They all need you too much.''

''You can see it better than I can,'' he responded, his voice gruff.

''You're the backbone of the Star Four, Jud. Maybe it used to be your father, but somewhere along the way it became you. And it could be he's having trouble accepting that.''

He didn't know if what Mariah said made sense. He was too close to it to tell.

As they sat there, the heat from his hand on her knee seeming to spread all around them, she asked, ''Is Shelby going to keep quiet about my pregnancy? I didn't mean to blurt it out like that—''

''Yes, you did. But I should have told her myself. Before last night. And I should have told *you* there's nothing between me and Shelby except a few good times. We haven't even had those for over eighteen months. When I took off, I didn't tell her I was leaving. After I got back, she was upset about it and I promised to take her to her party. I gave my word, Mariah.''

''Why didn't you just tell me that?''

''Because I'm not used to answering to anyone now. All my life, Dad was there, looking over my shoulder. While I was gone, I decided no one would ever do that to me again.''

"I see."

Her words were soft and understanding, and he wanted to kiss the shape of her lips and sink himself into her so badly he ached. But last night had taught him self-control was much more important than satisfying a need. He couldn't take the chance of chasing her off again. "So you'll come back to the ranch?"

"You really want me there?"

"Yes, I do."

She studied him for a long time until she took a deep breath and said, "All right. I just have to pack up my toothbrush and we can go."

The relief Jud felt made him almost feel happy. He hadn't felt happiness since he'd returned from Montana. Maybe this child was an answer to a lot of his questions.

Only time would tell.

Mariah felt Jud's gaze follow her as she helped Flo clear the table Sunday evening. The tension between them had eased some since he'd asked her to come back to the ranch. But the sparks dancing whenever they were in the same room still seemed ready to ignite at a moment's notice. Tonight, the lines around Jud's eyes cut deep and he looked tired. When the phone rang, Flo went to the kitchen to answer it. A few minutes later, Mariah set a stack of dishes in the sink.

Flo hung up the phone, looking troubled. "It's my

sister. Her husband has to go away on a business trip. He's looking for a new job, and she's afraid to stay alone. They live out in the middle of nowhere.''

"Where does she live?''

"Near Lufkin. She wants me to drive there tomorrow. But I hate to leave all of you in the lurch. She thinks he'll be gone till Friday.''

"Go,'' Mariah encouraged her. "We'll be fine. I can cook and do laundry.''

"Are you sure you want to take that on?'' Jud asked from the doorway.

At least he was asking instead of telling her not to consider it. "I'll keep it simple. No fancy stuff. Scrambled eggs for breakfast, except for Thatcher. Sandwiches for lunch. Meat and vegetables for supper. And a few loads of wash. It's less than a week.''

"We can get someone from town to help out.''

If he was concerned about her and the baby, she had to respect that. "Tell you what. Let me try it and if it's too much, I'll let you know.''

He came closer to her, his gaze lingering on her mouth then lifting to her eyes. "You won't let pride stand in your way?''

She shook her head. "I promise if I need help, I'll tell you.''

Reaching out his hand as if to touch her, he abruptly pulled it back. "I'm going to take a shower. Flo, if I don't see you before you leave, you take care.''

When Mack and Thatcher came into the kitchen, Flo explained about her sister. Mariah offered to finish cleaning up if Flo wanted to pack so she could get an early start in the morning.

Thatcher had gone out for a walk while Mariah closed the dishwasher and switched it on. Then she decided to gather laundry so she could start it first thing in the morning. Going upstairs to her room, she gathered a pair of dusty jeans and T-shirts she'd dumped in her closet. She didn't hear the shower running and figured Jud was in his room.

His door stood ajar. When she raised her hand to knock, she glimpsed his bare legs on the bed, and she dropped the clothes in her arms. They brushed to the floor, pushing the door open wider. Jud was sprawled on his back, only black briefs covering him, while one arm rested across his forehead. She froze, unable to look away.

Up between four and five in the morning, not going to bed until midnight, engaging in physical work most of the day, she wasn't surprised he'd conked out at week's end. But thoughts of Jud's work week flittered out of her mind as the sight of his hard, muscled body mesmerized her. His chest hair was so thick, she longed to sift her fingers through it. She took a step closer, aching to brush the lock of still shower-damp hair from his forehead. Before she could stop herself, her gaze drifted down his body, over his navel to…

His body stirred, and fascinated, she watched.

"If you know what's good for you, Mariah, you'll leave now." His deep voice was husky.

She couldn't make her feet move and her heart raced.

"Unless you want the same thing to happen that happened in the barn in February," he added.

Maybe it was his slightly mocking tone or the tinge of regret in his voice, but one or the other made her fire back, "Well, if it did, at least I wouldn't have to worry about getting pregnant this time, would I?" Without waiting for his answer, she swept up the clothes on the floor and closed the door.

Why was he fighting the attraction between them so hard? For his good or for hers?

Judson Whitmore was a more complicated man than J.T. ever could be. Would he always remain a stranger to her?

Gray clouds blew across the sky Monday afternoon, stacking up, bumping into each other, until Jud knew the storm wouldn't pass over. It had been brewing all day. Going to an outside spigot, he turned it on and splashed water over his face and around the back of his neck. The sun might have taken a day off, but the humidity hadn't.

When he heard the crunch of tires, he swiped loose drops of water from his neck and went around the barn. The van that had drawn up at the house was unfamiliar...

Suddenly he recognized the man who climbed out and he broke into a smile. Luke. He'd seen him about two months ago when he'd delivered a horse to Christopher in Connecticut. But it was good to see him here, on the ranch where they'd spent summers together as kids. Jud hurried his stride. So did Luke. Grinning, they clasped forearms and clapped each other on the back.

"What are you doing here?" Jud asked, noting Luke was as fit as ever. At six foot two, his cousin had always carried his height as if he was proud of it. Although he sat at a desk nine or ten months out of the year, he also rode, played tennis and worked out.

"My project for this summer is in a small town near Abilene. I figured I'd stop on the way."

"What are you working on this year?" Coming from wealth, Luke ran his family's foundation. It had been set up to give worthwhile causes, and sometimes individuals, a boost. With a degree in structural engineering, every summer he traded his suit for jeans and a hard hat, supervised a job, and stayed in touch with how real people lived.

"A library. The town's old one burned down and they didn't have the money to rebuild."

Thunder grumbled and the wind picked up. Jud glanced toward the house.

"Is Uncle Thatcher inside?"

"No...uh...he's down at the tack room. How long are you planning to stay?"

Luke cocked his head and studied Jud curiously. "A few days. Unless that's a problem."

"No. Of course not. It's just..." The wind buffeted him much the same way his reactions to Mariah did. "Have you talked to Christopher?"

"Not recently. Since he and Jenny renewed their vows, they're in a world of their own."

"Two weeks ago I called him. Remember the girl I told you about?"

"The twenty-one-year-old virgin in Montana?" Jud had confided in both of his cousins about his poor judgement.

"Yeah. She's here. And she's pregnant."

Luke's brows arched. "What are you going to do?"

Jud swore. "Why does everybody think I have to *do* something?"

"Maybe because you're not a man who stands still while life rolls over him. Is she here permanently?"

"She's twenty-one. What does she know about permanence? She's still dreaming about seeing the pyramids!"

With a rumble of thunder and a gust of wind they couldn't ignore, rain dripped from the clouds, then came down steadier. Jud motioned toward the house. "Let's go inside."

Luke stopped at the van and pulled out a suitcase.

By the time he reached the porch behind Jud, his T-shirt was wet and his jeans damp.

The aroma of something sweet and baked wound around Jud as he stepped into the kitchen. The smell of summer rain and damp earth blew in the door with them. Mariah had opened the oven and was removing something from it. The foot-long glass dish looked tempting.

"I thought you weren't going to make anything fancy." The scene in his room last night played over in his mind. He'd decided to close his eyes for a few minutes after his shower and had dozed off. When Mariah had dropped the clothes at his door, he'd awakened. The knowledge she was looking at him the way he wanted to look at her had aroused him. He'd had to chase her off or the situation would have become more complicated than it already was.

She set the dish on a rack on the counter and closed the oven door. "This isn't fancy. It's just peaches and cinnamon, a few oats and a little flour. I thought your dad might like it."

Dropping his suitcase by the table, Luke stood waiting.

Jud waved at him. "This is my cousin, Luke Hobart. He'll be staying a few days. Luke, Mariah Roswell."

Always the gentleman, Luke crossed to her and extended his hand. "Hi. It seems funny to see anyone in the kitchen but Flo."

Mariah accepted his overture and gave his hand a shake. "Flo's away."

With a glance over his shoulder at his cousin, Luke said, "I don't want to cause you more work. I can stay in town or in the bunkhouse..."

She smiled at him. "Don't be silly. One more mouth won't make a difference."

Feeling the need to make sure Mariah wasn't overworked, Jud reminded her, "I told you we can get someone from town to help out."

"And I told *you* that's not necessary." She looked squarely at Luke. "Do you know why I'm here?"

"Jud told me you're pregnant," Luke answered, trying to bite back a grin.

She gave a sigh of relief. "Good. Then we don't have to tiptoe around it." Turning her attention back to Jud, she said, "I'll go up and make sure one of the extra rooms is ready. Does it matter which one Luke sleeps in?"

"No."

After another smile for Luke to tell him he was welcome, she went into the living room and up the steps.

Jud took a carton of juice from the refrigerator, waiting for his cousin to say something. When he didn't, Jud asked, "Well?"

"Well what? You expect an opinion after a handshake and a few sentences?"

"No, I don't want an opinion. But I know you'll have something to say. You always do."

"Not this time."

Something in Luke's voice made Jud take notice. "Why not?"

"I might date a different woman every weekend and look like I'm having a good time, and most nights I am, but when it comes to something this serious— you and a woman and a baby—I think I should stay out of it."

"That's not like you."

"I was wrong about Jenny."

After an automobile accident which had left Christopher's wife Jenny with a memory loss, both Christopher and Luke had suspected she'd had an affair before her accident. Although he was cynical about women, Jud had always liked Jenny, and gut instinct had told him she'd never be unfaithful to her husband. She *had* been hiding a secret, but he'd been right about her fidelity and commitment to Christopher.

Jud knew Luke felt badly about his lack of faith. "Evidence stacked up against her."

"But it didn't sway you. And it's not just Jenny. I've never said anything, but Stacey and I didn't have the trust between us we needed. She might be alive now if we did."

"Don't go beating yourself up over something you had no power over. Cancer took her. You couldn't stop it."

"No, but if she had told me about her symptoms sooner…"

"Luke, your wife died over three years ago." More gently he added, "You have to let it go."

Luke took two glasses from the cupboard. "That's easier said than done."

After pouring the orange juice, Jud sat at the table. Silence stretched until Luke asked, "How do you feel about Mariah being here?"

"I'm not sure what she wants."

"A father for her child?"

"Maybe. More likely she wants more than she's had. She and her mom skimped all their lives. I don't want to marry her and wake up a month later realizing she's just used me to get lifelong security or a checkbook of her own."

Snagging a chair with his foot, Luke sat across from Jud. "I like summers when no one looks at me as if I can do them a favor, as if money solves problems easier than good sense. Pretending to be an ordinary guy gives me freedom I don't have otherwise."

"Yeah, but the responsibility's always waiting. You can pretend, but you can't forget or deny who you are."

Luke turned around his glass. "I guess not. But Uncle Thatcher's heart attack trapped you here. Now you just want to make sure marriage doesn't trap you besides."

"You got that right."

* * *

When Mariah put a fresh set of towels on the guest room bed for Luke, she felt a fluttering sensation in her...stomach? For the past week she'd been aware of the feeling, but as she put her hand over her tummy and felt the thickening of her waist—she'd kept her jeans unsnapped under her knit top this past week—a new knowing settled over her. The fluttering was the baby!

Excited, she went to the dresser mirror and lifted her top. Lovingly she moved her hand from right to left over her midriff. Her baby was moving inside of her. She had to tell Jud.

Hurrying down the stairs, she was almost at the kitchen doorway when she heard Jud's cousin say, "But Uncle Thatcher's heart attack trapped you here. Now you just want to make sure marriage doesn't trap you besides."

Jud's agreement stopped her from taking another step. He thought she wanted to trap him. He saw marriage as a trap. And a baby...?

Turning on her heels, she went back upstairs.

Shirtless, hauling bales of hay off a flatbed the following afternoon, Jud wondered about Mariah's quietness last evening. Yesterday, after the sky had cleared, he and Luke had gone riding, revisiting old haunts, remembering teenage shenanigans. Mariah had handled his cousin's arrival as if it was no bother. But after dinner she'd retired to her room. It wasn't like her.

If she wasn't feeling well, he wished she'd tell him. But her color was good, her appetite healthy. She was just…subdued.

Thunder grumbled and the wind picked up again as Jud hoisted the last bale into the barn, shrugged into his shirt, then made his way to the arena where Luke was watching Mack work a three-year-old. Yesterday's storm hadn't amounted to much. But with the bilious black clouds piling up, this one could be worse than the others.

A shot of lightning streaked the sky and cracked real close. Moments later, Jud heard a shout and turned to look over his shoulder.

Thatcher waved his hat and yelled, "It's Mariah."

Mariah? Wasn't she over in the pen? His father was beckoning from the pasture and Jud took off at a run.

When he reached the high grass, Thatcher looked worried. "She said she's okay. But I told her to stay put. She was in with the yearlings. When the lightning snapped, one of them reared up and knocked her down."

"Is she hurt?"

"Not as I could see. But it was a pretty hard tumble that knocked the breath out of her. Carl had ridden in from the north pasture. I told him to stay with her while I found you."

Jud saw Mariah, standing now, outside the fence. As he rushed up to her, he saw she looked pale.

"Just a little fall," she said but she looked as worried as he felt.

Without warning, he scooped her up in his arms. "I'm calling the doctor." He started walking, not paying attention to the wind whipping his shirt.

"Everything's probably fine…"

"We're going to make sure," he said in a tone that told her not to argue.

After he laid her on the sofa in the house, her hand protectively went to her stomach.

"What? Are you having cramps?" The thought of anything happening to this child…to her…

"No," she was quick to assure him.

He saw the outline of the snap of her jeans under her top. It was open. He realized what an idiot he'd been, not noticing she was wearing her shirts over her waistband, not tucked in. Her clothes were probably getting too tight. She'd said something once about making maternity clothes.…

Unsettled, he said gruffly, "I'll call the doctor."

Jud wanted Dr. Thomas to come out to the ranch. Since she had appointments into early evening, that was impossible. But she told him she'd fit Mariah in if he brought her to the office.

Luke had come in while he was talking to the doctor and with a few words from Thatcher discovered what was happening. He pulled a set of keys from his jeans. "Take the van. She'll be more comfortable than in your truck."

All of the vehicles on the ranch were trucks of one sort or another. With a nod of gratitude, Jud buttoned and tucked in his shirt, then took Luke's keys.

Rain poured down as he insisted on carrying Mariah to the van once he'd parked it close to the house. The silence as he drove was only broken by the pelting on the windshield and the hum of the air conditioner. He hated the feeling in his stomach. It was the same one that had lodged there when he'd gotten news of his dad's heart attack, and it had never dissipated completely. Jud hated feeling powerless, but as he glanced at Mariah and saw her bite her lip, he knew there was nothing he could do about it at the moment.

When he reached Dr. Thomas's office and went around to Mariah's door, she'd already opened it. "You're *not* carrying me inside."

The determination on her face made him hold out his hand to her to help her down and hover over her as they walked the short distance to the medical offices complex. They didn't have to wait long, but every moment seemed like a year. When a nurse took Mariah back to an examining room, Jud shifted restlessly and watched the closed door.

About fifteen minutes later, the nurse opened the door and beckoned to him. He removed his hat and crossed to her.

"Miss Roswell said you might like to be present during her sonogram."

He jumped at the chance. "Yes, ma'am, I would."

She smiled and gestured for him to follow her.

In his boots and jeans and work shirt, he felt totally out of place in the midst of white uniforms and pale blue walls with flowered borders. But none of that mattered as he entered a room where Mariah lay on a table by a machine with a monitor.

The doctor stood by Mariah's side. "She's fine. Babies are well protected against bumps and even minor falls. But I thought you both might feel better if you could see him or her."

His sense of relief enabled him to take a deep breath, his first in the last hour or so. Mariah wore a soft cotton gown pulled up above her navel. A sheet covered her from her pelvic area down. Her tummy wasn't flat as it used to be. It was slightly rounded and the feeling in his chest when he looked at it made his heart pump faster.

The doctor smoothed some kind of jelly over Mariah's stomach, then took a wand-like instrument over her belly as she stared at the screen.

There was a whooshing sound, and as Jud stared at the monitor, the doctor pointed to a tiny form. "There's your baby."

Jud couldn't take his eyes from the gray waves, the fetus that was his flesh and blood.

Dr. Thomas slowly moved the wand. "Everything

looks good. We're on target with the delivery date.'' She smiled at Mariah. ''But then you were sure when the child was conceived. Have you felt movement yet?''

''This weekend.'' Mariah's voice was low and husky. ''I might have even felt it before then but it wasn't until Saturday I realized what it was.''

She'd felt the baby alive inside her! At that moment, Jud envied her more than he ever imagined he could.

''Can you tell if it's a boy or a girl?'' Jud asked.

When the doctor looked at Mariah, she gave a nod that she'd like to know too.

''It's too soon to tell for sure.'' Dr. Thomas moved the wand for a while, then said, ''I can't guarantee I'm right at eighteen weeks, but my best guess would be it's a boy.''

All Jud's life he'd fought to take pride in himself and his accomplishments, separate from his father's. He'd fought to find a space of his own, a life that would satisfy him, not someone else. But he'd never felt the pride he experienced at this moment, the sense that maybe now he knew why he was here and his purpose for being.

This child, this heir, his son *or* daughter…

A few minutes later, the doctor removed the wand from Mariah's tummy.

Jud cleared his throat and composed his thoughts. ''Should Mariah rest today?''

''It won't hurt her to pamper herself today. Or another day when she doesn't have a fall to contend with. I don't expect any problems. But babies can surprise you. If you have any symptoms at all you don't understand, or if there's cramping or spotting, call me immediately. Otherwise, I'll see you in a few weeks. Take your time getting dressed.''

With encouraging smiles, the doctor and nurse left the room.

Jud had never known Mariah to be so quiet as she had been the last day or so, and he wondered if with the movement of the baby, the reality of motherhood was taking hold. He stood by her side as she pulled her gown down over her stomach. ''Why didn't you tell me you felt the baby move?''

Hesitation wasn't like Mariah, either. But she didn't answer him immediately. Finally snatching the sheet and holding it at her waist while she swung her legs over the side of the table, she said, ''I was going to. But when I came downstairs you and Luke were talking about your dad's heart attack and marriage, and I didn't think you'd want to know.''

Her eyes glistened softly as if everything that had happened had caught up with her. He remembered his conversation with Luke, talking about marriage as a trap. Since he'd seen his baby on the monitor, since he'd realized the only way he might keep both the child and Mariah safe was to keep them by his side, he knew what he had to do.

''You were wrong. I want to know everything about the baby. And I want more than that. I want you to marry me. How about it, Mariah?''

Chapter Seven

The sheet almost slipped through Mariah's fingers. He was asking her to marry him? After not wanting to feel trapped? After suspecting her motives? After acting as if he expected her to be a duty rather than a pleasure?

"You can't be serious!"

"I'm very serious."

"You were totally against the idea a couple of weeks ago."

"That was then. This is now. You're carrying the heir to the Star Four."

"As I was when I arrived. The doctor said there's no guarantee this child is a boy, so if you changed your mind because of that…"

"I changed my mind because this is *my* decision to make, not my father's."

There was no talk of love here, or even of need. Would he regret asking her an hour from now? "Maybe you'd better sleep on it."

"Mariah…"

"I mean it, Jud. We both got scared by the fall. Let's wait till morning to talk about marriage again."

For a second he frowned, and she thought he might get angry. But he looked at her sitting there in the skimpy gown and sheet, then lodged his hat back on his head. "All right. We'll talk about it in the morning. I'll be in the waiting room." Then he gave her a smile like one of those he'd charmed her with in Montana. "Unless you need help getting dressed."

If they married, would he expect her to be a wife in every sense of the word? Don't think about it yet, she warned herself. "I can manage," she responded, smoothing the sheet over her lap.

His smile still lingered as he opened the door and left the room.

They didn't talk about marriage again on the drive back to the ranch, or during the evening as Thatcher grilled steaks so she could rest rather than cook, or before bed as they all sat on the porch, breathing in the scents of summer, rain and dusk. Luke and Jud spoke of years past, and Thatcher related a few anecdotes about the three cousins sharing mischief as well as chores. Every once in a while Jud and Luke exchanged a look that made her wonder if Luke was aware of the proposal.

She thought about it, and she tried *not* thinking about it in case Jud changed his mind. Turning in before the men, she heard Jud and Luke mount the steps a few hours later. The creaking of Jud's bed as he settled for the night gave her a tummy-curling feeling. Maybe soon she'd be sharing that bed with him. Visions of their first time together kept her awake and then invaded brief dreams.

When the sun came up, she quickly showered and dressed, nervous yet hopeful her dreams could come true—a husband to love, a home, a baby. What more could she want?

She sat in her room and gazed out the window until she heard Jud stirring. His footsteps echoed in the hall as he made a trip to the bathroom and back. Then she opened her door…and waited.

As he stopped in her doorway, she didn't think he'd ever looked more handsome. His plaid shirt was faded and soft, and he'd rolled back the sleeves. The black hair on his forearms was masculine and rough and reminded her of the hair on his chest. His work jeans were white at the knees and the fly. He was every inch the rugged cowboy—a mixture of the rakish J.T. and the duty-bound Jud. She loved him.

"Get any sleep?" he asked with a morning raspiness that gave her an excited tingling up her spine.

"Some. How about you?"

"I slept. Because I know what I want. I haven't

changed my mind, Mariah. I want to take care of you and the baby the right way. Will you marry me?''

The excitement gave way to disappointment that this decision was so matter-of-fact for him. She didn't hear or see any feeling, and she wondered what kind of marriage they could have. "What would you expect of me as your wife?''

His blue eyes deepened. "If you're asking if I want you in my bed, I sure do. We'll figure out the rest as it comes.''

She stood and walked toward him. "I'll marry you, Jud. And I promise I'll do everything I can to build a good life with you.''

After studying her with an intensity that took her breath away, he said, "I'll tell Dad. I'd like to do this as soon as possible. After we got back yesterday, I made some calls. We can get the license today, wait seventy-two hours, then get married. I figured we can set it all up for Saturday. I found a minister who can come to the ranch in the evening.''

"Don't I need a birth certificate or something? That could take time…''

"All you need is a valid driver's license.''

"I have that.''

"Great. So are we getting married Saturday evening?''

She wanted to marry Jud, but so quickly, without tender words, without time to plan, without her mother… But she couldn't hesitate now. She had to look forward. "Do you mind if I call my mother? I doubt if she can come on such short notice."

"I'll fly her in if she wants to be here."

"I can't ask you to do that."

"I'm offering. The ceremony will probably last ten minutes and it won't be anything fancy, but if you want Edda here, she should be here."

"I'd rather have her come when the baby's born," Mariah said softly, afraid to ask for too much. If she showed him she wasn't after his money, or just his name, if she loved him and their child the best she could love, maybe he'd eventually love her back.

"It doesn't have to be one or the other. She's welcome when the baby's born, too."

"Thank you."

He looked embarrassed. "No thanks necessary. I'll go down and prepare Dad so he doesn't squeeze the stuffing out of you when you come down. How do you feel?"

"I feel fine. I was more scared yesterday than anything."

Coming closer to her, he lifted her chin and gazed into her eyes. "I want to get married quickly for the baby, to avoid rumors and gossip. But I also want you in my bed. Then maybe I can think straight again."

When he lowered his head, he took her lips, then possessed her with a deep, scalding kiss that left her breathless. As he stepped away and walked down the hall, his words finally sank in. He was marrying her for the baby and for sex.

Was she making the biggest mistake of her life?

Although Jud had "prepared" his father, Thatcher still squeezed the stuffing out of her. His joy was obvious as he murmured in her ear, "You'll be good for him."

Wondering if that was true, she'd accepted Luke's more tempered congratulations, not knowing what one of Jud's best friends was thinking. The two cousins were close, that was apparent in their silent looks, the camaraderie between them. Luke would evidently support whatever his cousin chose to do.

The men had decided to go to the bunkhouse kitchen for breakfast so she didn't have to cook. No amount of arguing would change their minds. After they left, she dialed Montana. She'd written to her mother often since she'd arrived because she knew she would worry. When Edda answered, Mariah plunged right in. "Jud asked me to marry him. This coming Saturday."

Edda was quiet for a few seconds. "Is this what you want?"

"I love him, Mama."

"Does he love you?"

She hesitated too long.

"Your father and I didn't have much, but we had that."

"He cares about me, Mama. I can tell. It's just hard for him to admit what he feels."

"Just so you're not fooling yourself."

Mariah prayed she wasn't. "He said he'll fly you in if you want to come."

"You know I'd like nothing better, honey, but..."

"What's wrong?"

"There's things going on here. Mr. Hopkins doesn't confide in me so I'm not sure what they are. But a man was here with a calculator and a legal pad. And another stranger in a suit. I think he was a real estate agent."

"Ask Mr. Hopkins, Mama."

"I can't do that! It's not my place. If there's something I need to know, he'll tell me. But it's just a feeling I have that I'd better not leave right now. You know I'd like to be there."

She was disappointed, but she did understand. Her mother had to do what was best for her. "Jud said you can come when the baby's born."

"Oh, I'd like that. And I promise nothing will keep me away then. Are you gonna be all right?"

"Sure I am. The ceremony won't take long and there's nothing planned afterwards. Nothing's going to really change." Except she'd be Jud's wife.

She'd just hung up the phone when Jud came into the kitchen. "Are you sure you're feeling all right?"

"Positive."

"Is your mom coming?"

"She can't right now."

After a speculative look, he said, "I'll be ready to go into town around ten. If you're up to it, I thought we'd do some shopping after we get the license. You can buy something for the wedding and clothes that fit so you don't have to walk around with your jeans unsnapped."

"I told you I can make—"

"If you want to make things for the baby, that's fine. But my wife doesn't have to make her own clothes. You can find what you need while I run errands. I'll settle up when I come back for you."

"Jud, I like to sew and I'm good at it." One look at him told her he was remembering the black dress.

"You can go to the fabric shop another time. I have to get back for some appointments this afternoon."

"Shelby?" she asked.

"It's just for training, Mariah. We have the Summer Classic in a couple of weeks. And before she hears it somewhere else, I want to tell her about the wedding."

There was really nothing she could say to that. She wouldn't let her jealousy drive him away any more than she would drive him away with demands for more than he wanted to give.

The quarter moon shone a path of light across the grass in front of the house as Mariah rocked on the swing. Cicadas chirped and a cow lowed in the distance. It was almost 3:00 a.m. and everyone else was asleep. Tomorrow, rather today, she was getting married. She had every right to have insomnia. Since Jud's proposal and their trip into town for the license, her world had...tilted.

A noise in the kitchen alerted her to someone else's presence. Glad she'd dressed in a new set of shorts and a top, she waited, hoping Jud couldn't sleep either. Other than the drive to and from Tyler, they hadn't spent any time alone. They'd gone into town for the Fourth of July fireworks last night, but Thatcher and Luke had come along. With the usual work on the ranch, and both Thatcher and Luke in the house, privacy seemed to be a dream. Not that Jud had indicated he wanted to spend time with her other than that last fiery kiss...

She knew immediately the shadowed figure in the doorway wasn't Jud. Luke opened the screen and came out onto the porch. "Nice night," he said.

"It's a beautiful night."

The swing creaked as he sat beside her. "I heard you come downstairs. And when you didn't come back up—"

She sighed. "You were worried. I have so many people to worry about me..."

"That you have to sneak out at night to get some peace and quiet," Luke finished with a smile in his voice. "I thought staying until after the wedding was a good idea. Maybe it wasn't."

Clasping his arm, she assured him, "Jud wants you here."

"And you want what he wants?" His question was part curious, part mocking.

Dropping her hand, she answered, "I want what's good for him. You're good for him. He relaxes when he's around you. He was like that with me in Montana. Here, there's this tension between us. Maybe after tomorrow it will be different."

"Wedding vows won't solve anything, Mariah."

"No, but I believe Jud's a man of his word, and I won't make a promise I can't keep. Vows will be a bond between us."

"That bond will only be as strong as the two of you make it."

Luke sounded as if he knew, as if a bond he'd shared hadn't been strong enough. Before she could monitor it, she let the question foremost in her mind pop out. "Do you think Jud will ever let his guard down enough to love me?"

"Mariah…"

"You *know* him, Luke. Why does he protect himself so well?"

"He doesn't trust easily."

"He doesn't trust women. Why not?"

"Jud should tell you himself."

"You and I both know Jud won't tell me."

The silence lasted so long she didn't think Luke would respond. But then he shifted toward her, and even in the shadows she could see his serious expression.

"Did you know Jud's mother died a year after he was born?"

She nodded.

"He grew up feeling his mother left him and his father was always taking him to task. He'd never admit it, and Thatcher would deny that he was ever too hard, but he was, and Jud grew a real tough skin. Though *he'd* deny it, he admires Thatcher as much as he's frustrated by him."

"They're two of a kind," she murmured.

"Yes, they are. And that's one reason why when Thatcher was betrayed, Jud felt betrayed, too. When Jud was thirteen, Thatcher fell in love again. Or lust. Or something. But the woman was out to take him for all he was worth. Even at thirteen, Jud could see it, though his dad couldn't. Thatcher thought Jud was jealous that he was giving time, attention and money to someone else."

"Jud's not like that."

"You're right, he's not. But he was determined to make Thatcher see the truth. He saw his dad's fiancée ride out one day. A hand followed her. Jud caught them in a lean-to in a winter pasture…intimately connected, should we say. They said Jud was lying and denied it. And Thatcher wanted to believe his fiancée."

"And neither Jud nor Thatcher has ever forgotten it."

"Nope. Thatcher only believed Jud when another hand came to him out of loyalty and told him he'd enjoyed his fiancée's pleasures, too. Thatcher broke his engagement, kept the hand on who was honest, and never spoke about it again. Add to that experience the women who have tried to entice Jud into bed hoping they'll eventually win the crown of Mrs. Judson Whitmore, and you've got one cynical cowboy."

"He wasn't like that when I met him. His eyes twinkled, he knew how to laugh. But I think he can be that way here, too, if he'd give himself a chance. Maybe this child will bring the laughter back to his eyes."

"Maybe you will." Luke sounded sincere.

"I never meant to trap him," she murmured.

"Give him time, Mariah. When he realizes you want to build a life with him, not just take his name, maybe he'll let that guard down."

"Then maybe he'll fall in love?"

"Then maybe he'll fall in love."

Suddenly fatigue overtook her and she had to yawn. Standing, she said, "I think I can fall asleep now. Thanks for telling me about Jud. It helps me understand."

"He deserves some happiness, Mariah. I think you and the baby might be what's been missing from his life."

Something made her ask, "What about you? Are you happy?"

"Sure, I am."

But the way he said it made her wonder. "Do you have someone to love?"

His words were slow in coming. "I did once. But... Loving isn't simple, and I'm not sure I'll ever be ready for the complications of it again. I have people who care about me. Work I like. It's enough."

"Maybe for now. But if you're the kind of man I think you are, you'll eventually want more."

He laughed. "Jud didn't tell me you could read fortunes."

"I can't. I just try to see with my heart as well as with my eyes." Knowing she'd said enough, she opened the screen door. "Good night, Luke. I'll see you in the morning."

"Good night, Mariah. I hope your wedding day brings you everything you're wishing for."

Closing the door, she hoped it would, too.

The preparation pulsating all around Mariah made her nervous. Flo, who had just returned that morning, told her Thatcher had ordered a catered buffet for after the ceremony. Two white canopies had been set up in the back yard—one for the ceremony, the other covering a long table and chairs and the buffet table. A delivery person carried large bouquets of pink-and-white flowers to the stands under the canopies.

Mariah bet Jud was having a fit at Thatcher's high-handedness. But she hadn't seen him all day so she didn't know.

Around five, a car drew up outside. Suddenly Jud and Luke and Thatcher appeared around it, talking and laughing with the couple that emerged. Mariah went out on the porch, knowing Jud was expecting his cousin Christopher.

A handsome man dressed in a striped polo shirt and navy shorts looked over at her. He bent his head to the pretty, black-haired woman beside him who held a silver-wrapped package in her arms. With a smile, she gazed in Mariah's direction. The group walked toward the house, Jud leading the way. Luke carried a suitcase he'd taken from the back seat of the car.

Jud's gaze passed over Mariah's new jeans and loose top. She'd chosen clothes that would last throughout her pregnancy and they felt big now. As always, she wondered what he was thinking. As she grew bigger would he still find her attractive?

The question became future food for thought as Jud said, "This is my cousin, Christopher, and his wife Jenny."

She shook both their hands.

Christopher arched his brows at Jud and smiled. Jenny handed her the present. "We didn't know what you needed so we got something impractical you can hand down to your children."

"Should I open it now?" Mariah asked.

"Go ahead," Jud said.

Sitting on the swing, Mariah pulled off the bow. Then she unwrapped the box and lifted the lid. Brushing aside the packing materials, she reached in and pulled out a crystal bowl. Her name and Jud's as well as the date were inscribed in the center of an intricate etched design that swirled around the crystal dish.

Tears came to her eyes. "It's wonderful! I've never held anything so beautiful. Thank you."

Thatcher came up on the porch. "Don't you think it's about time we all get ready for a wedding? The photographer said he'd be here around six-thirty."

"Photographer?" Jud asked with a frown.

"We need pictures to remember this day. You don't have to do anything but show up, though a smile now and then wouldn't hurt."

"We wanted to keep it simple," Jud reminded his father, his lips tight.

"It's simple," Thatcher said, throwing up his hands. "A few people, flowers, food. Nothing could be simpler."

Luke and Christopher exchanged grins while Jud shook his head and explained, "The men are getting dressed down at Mack's. That way you, Jenny and Flo can have the run of the house."

After Mariah set the bowl on the sideboard in the dining room and the men had taken their clothes to Mack's, she and Jenny took turns in the upstairs bathroom getting ready while Flo dressed downstairs and took care of last-minute preparations. Mariah found herself liking Christopher's wife a lot—she was warm, friendly and kept up a running conversation to ease Mariah's jitters....

Until she walked around to the back of the house and saw Jud standing under the canopy in his western-cut black suit and hat, a most serious expression on his face.

Thatcher waited for her and held out his arm to walk her up the short aisle. Her left hand tightened on her flowers and she slipped her right into his elbow.

Jud hadn't seen the dress she'd chosen for their wedding. The clerk had already bagged it when he'd returned from his errands to settle the bill. It was off-white, gauzy, with smocking across the high waist. Soft gathers fell to her calves. The square neck was trimmed in écru lace as were the flowing short sleeves. Earlier, she'd snitched baby's breath and three sweetheart roses from the arrangements. When she'd formed a small ponytail from the upswept sides of her hair, she'd woven the flowers into it.

Jud's gaze swept over her from head to toe then came back to her face. She gave him a tentative smile, and his features relaxed a bit. When Thatcher reached Jud, he took her hand from his arm and placed it in his son's. Jud's fingers were warm and firm and strong, as was everything else about him.

The minister smiled down at them and welcomed

Jud and Mariah's guests who were limited to the hands, Flo and Mack, Luke, Christopher and Jenny. Mariah suddenly missed her mother desperately.

Jud took off his hat and handed it to Luke. Then he squeezed her hand and murmured close to her ear, "I'm sure your mom is here with you in spirit."

She felt closer to him at that moment than she had since they'd made love in Montana.

With the scent of roses and grass surrounding her, Mariah was more aware of Jud standing beside her than the minister's words...until the man asked them to respond "I do" to their wedding vows. Jud's voice was low but firm. Hers came from her heart.

When he produced a gold wedding band from his inside jacket pocket and slipped it on her finger, she held her breath.

"With this ring, I thee wed," he said, gazing into her eyes.

She wanted to see into his soul. But she couldn't. He wore protective armor she couldn't penetrate. Turning to Jenny, who was holding Jud's ring, Mariah took it. She'd been pleased when he'd shown her the two gold bands he'd bought, exactly alike except for their size. Hers had fit perfectly. She'd been surprised he wanted to wear one. But exchanging rings made the promise of their marriage and the bond she prayed for between them more of a reality.

Sending up another prayer for their future, she slid

the band onto his finger, repeating, "With this ring, I thee wed."

The minister's words and the final blessing passed quickly. When he proclaimed to those gathered that she and Jud were husband and wife and they could kiss, she looked up at her husband, hoping to see a vision of their life together in his eyes. But she only glimpsed sparks of desire as he bent his head and took her in his arms.

The heat of his body was a craving that was more demanding than chocolate or pickles or fresh peaches on vanilla ice cream. His breath seared her lips before his mouth covered hers. She opened to him immediately, and her pulse quickened as his tongue thrust into her mouth, teased her with erotic caresses, then withdrew.

When he raised his head, she admired his control. Only the flush high on his cheekbones told her he'd like to finish what he'd started. He took his hat from Luke and lodged it back on his head. With her knees shaking, she lifted her flowers from Jenny's lap and smiled at their guests.

As everyone congratulated them and the caterer readied the buffet, Mariah wondered about the wisdom of having a reception after the wedding. She'd be willing to bet there was only one thing on the mind of the bride and groom at most weddings, and it wasn't making small talk or eating a piece of wedding cake. But Thatcher seemed to be thriving on tradition and ritual. His toast to their happiness couldn't have been more sincere. Yet she didn't feel united to Jud. She didn't feel truly married. Maybe they just needed time together, but what she wanted most at the moment was to simply be alone with him.

The red-orange sun dipped behind the live oaks and finally the horizon when the photographer left. As Mariah finished her cake and sipped her punch, Flo came up to Jud and said, "Everything's ready."

He nodded, then stood and placed his hand on Mariah's shoulder. "And now if all you good folks will excuse us, we'll be leaving until tomorrow afternoon."

"Leaving?" Thatcher's voice held surprise.

"Yep. Mariah and I will be spending the night somewhere more private. Flo has the number in case of an emergency, but she's sworn to secrecy so don't try to con her into giving it to you." He squeezed Mariah's shoulder.

"But I don't have anything ready…"

He whispered into her ear, "You don't need anything tonight, and Flo packed a bag with clothes for tomorrow. Unless you'd rather not go…"

"I love the idea of a honeymoon night," she murmured. "Of course, I want to go." She rose to her feet.

Just then, someone came around the side of the house. It was Shelby Vance with a present in her hands. "Hi, y'all. Don't mean to intrude. I just wanted to wish the couple the best of luck."

Mariah knew better. The woman's eyes went to Jud and lingered. Then she approached him and handed him the present.

He set it on the table. "Thanks, Shelby. But we'll open it when we get back. We were just leaving." To Mariah he said, "I'll get the truck and pick you up out front." With a wave to everyone, he headed for the shed.

Smiling, Mariah pushed in her chair. "I'd better get my purse or he'll leave without me."

Thatcher's guffaw followed her to the kitchen. At the porch she realized Shelby had, too. She faced her and asked, "Is there something you wanted?"

Shelby slipped one hand into the back pocket of her white jeans. "Oh, yes. I just want you to know that after this baby's born, you'll no longer have a hold on Jud."

"We got married tonight, Shelby. That's a lifelong commitment."

"Don't fool yourself. And don't think just because there's a ring on your finger you won the prize. Jud married you to have legal rights to his child. In this county Whitmores can get whatever they want. And if he decides he doesn't want *you* but he wants sole custody of his child, that's what a judge will give him."

There should be no place for doubts on her wedding day. There should be no room for suspicions that Jud wanted his child but didn't want her. He was a man of his word, he was responsible, he was...a man who might feel trapped by his father and by her.

Not wanting Shelby to see her insecurities, she made her voice as confident as her expression. "You think what you want, Shelby. But the fact is that Jud chose *me*...not you. He put a ring on *my* finger. And I'm going to be the one sharing his bed."

Shelby looked unfazed. "You might be sharing his bed, but you're too young to have enough experience to please a man like Jud. He's *very* experienced. And in a little while when your belly sticks out, the memory of your wedding night might be all you have."

Not letting Shelby see that her arrow had hit a bull's-eye, Mariah returned, "You're wrong there. I'll still have a wedding ring, and I'll still be carrying Jud's baby. No matter what else happens, I'm the mother of the heir to the Star Four."

Without waiting for Shelby's response, knowing her parting shot had been her best, she went into the house for her purse, her hands shaking.

What if Jud *had* only married her to get legal rights to his child?

Chapter Eight

Jud had brought her to the best hotel in Tyler. At least it seemed that way as Mariah looked around the room at the quality of the furnishings, bedspread and drapes.

"This is nice," she said softly, noticing a world of differences between this room and the one she'd taken when she'd left the Star Four.

After depositing their suitcase on the luggage rack, Jud took off his hat and set it on the dresser. "I thought we deserved something nice tonight along with some privacy."

He'd left the jacket to his suit at the house. Now he unfastened the top button of his shirt and slid his string tie over his head, laying it on the dresser beside his hat. Then he crooked his finger at her. "Come here."

With her heart racing, she walked toward her new husband and stopped before him.

Fingering a lock of hair along her cheek, he gazed into her eyes. "I want you."

Already she was trembling, and he hadn't really touched her. More than anything, she wanted to tell him she loved him. But although she saw desire in his eyes, she couldn't see anything else, and she was afraid the words would become another barrier between them.

"What are you thinking, Mariah?"

His tone was gruff and she knew if she lied to him he'd know it. So she put one of her fears into words. "I'm wondering how long you'll want me. I'm going to gain weight—"

He slid his fingers under her hair and his thumbs stroked her neck. "Pregnant women are supposed to gain weight. Why don't you stop worrying about the future and start thinking about right now?"

Hadn't she longed for tonight? Wanted nothing more than to be with him like this? If she got greedy, she could lose it all. In time, if she loved Jud enough, maybe he'd come to love her, too.

Lifting her head, she brought her hands to his shoulders. "I *am* thinking about now."

The glow of the dresser light played on his face when he bent his head. He watched her as his lips came toward hers. When he was a breath away, she could feel the tension in his hands on her neck—a tension that had always vibrated between them. Now the anticipation of its release almost made her dizzy.

She thought he'd be hungry. She thought he'd demand a response. She thought fervor would outweigh gentleness. But she was wrong and very surprised. His lips hardly touched hers, and she realized the tension in his fingers came from restraint. When he brushed his mouth back and forth over hers, she slid her hands across his shoulders to explore. He practically whispered a kiss on her upper lip, and she wanted to melt at his feet. Her eyes closed and she waited for whatever came next.

Holding her head firmly, he nibbled on her lower lip, then kissed the point of her chin. "Everything's been too fast between us. We're going to take this slow."

The texture of his lips, the huskiness of his voice, the sure command of his hands suggested slow would be more exciting than fast ever could be.

Until he stopped altogether and raised his head. She felt the space between them as his hands slipped from her hair and she opened her eyes.

"What?" she asked, suddenly afraid he'd changed his mind about wanting her, about marrying her.

"I don't want to hurt the baby."

Tenderness for the man before her vied with all the other emotions he stirred up. "You won't. The doctor gave me a pamphlet the first time I went. As long as I'm not having any problems, we're not limited. In fact it can even help my muscles get ready for delivery.''

"It can?" Jud's eyes twinkled and his smile became rakish and sexy and satisfied all at the same time.

"It can," she said, deciding slow was fine but the anticipation was torture. She brought her fingers to his shirt buttons and started unfastening.

His smile turned into a grin. "Are you trying to tell me something?"

When his skin was exposed, she leaned forward and placed a kiss just below his collarbone. "Nope, I'm trying to show you something. I want you, too."

"Maybe slow isn't exactly what we need." His voice was thick, and he wrapped his arms around her, pulling her close.

With a kiss that was as delicious as it was hot, as seductive as it was satisfying, as deep as it was sensual, he backed her up closer to the bed. His hands passed up and down her back. Finally he caught her zipper and pulled it down its track. As their tongues cavorted, she laced her hands in his hair and held on.

Shelby's words haunted her. *You're too young to have enough experience to please a man like Jud. He's very experienced.* Holding no illusions about why they were here, Mariah knew Jud wanted to give and receive pleasure. Somehow she had to be his equal. Somehow she had to show him his fantasies were hers and she *could* satisfy him. Their marriage could depend on what happened tonight.

He broke the kiss to nuzzle her neck, and while he did, he brushed her dress from her shoulders. Experience. He knew exactly what he was doing. She'd have to rely on her instincts and pretend she did, too.

The pulse in Jud's temples pounded as he strove for control. Everything about Mariah filled his senses, riled his hormones, and confused the heck out of him. He'd never wanted a woman the way he wanted her. He'd never had a problem maintaining control. But ever since that night in Montana when the sparks between them had caught fire, he'd felt this need that wouldn't go away.

Spending the first night of their marriage in a house full of people had been out of the question. Not that Luke, Christopher and Jenny wouldn't have tried to give them privacy, but Thatcher... Jud could almost imagine his father standing outside the door, calling instructions!

Tonight, he'd wanted Mariah to himself.

Her dress caught between their bodies. Stepping back, he pushed it to the floor. She was wearing a long half slip, almost the same soft material as the dress. He couldn't keep from settling his hands on her bare midriff. She was warm and smooth and all he could think about was driving himself into her, but he took a deep breath and tugged the slip away from her waist, over her hips to the floor.

Adrenaline surged through him and, for the first time in his life, he could swear his knees were shaking. He watched, fascinated as Mariah unhooked her bra and pushed down her panties. She stood before him completely naked.

Her breasts were larger than a few months ago, and he reached out to touch one. As his thumb made a circle around her nipple, she closed her eyes. He smoothed his other hand over her tummy which was rounding. Her eyelids fluttered open and she looked at him.

"Our child," he murmured.

Her eyes glistened, and he scooped her up in his arms. After he laid her on the bed, she watched him undress. His body was hard and fit from the physical labor on the ranch, and he'd never thought much about it. But as her gaze dallied on him now, he was glad for the work that had sculpted his muscles. He'd never cared how he'd looked for a woman. But the desire in Mariah's eyes changed all that.

When he lay down beside her, she said, "I want to touch you."

Her boldness surprised him, though he supposed it shouldn't because everything about Mariah was unpredictable. "We're going to do a lot of touching and anything else that feels good."

As he shifted closer, she ran her hand up his chest through the hair until she came to his nipple. She brushed her thumb over it, and a shudder ran through him. Before he could take a breath, she'd brought her lips to him and teased the bud with her tongue.

He braced his hand on her shoulder. "Mariah."

"Don't you like it?" Her voice contained the worry in her eyes.

"I like it just fine. But you keep that up and this is going to be a short run."

"I just want to make you feel good…"

When her voice caught, he cupped her chin. She made him want and need so much that, most of the time, he pulled back as a defense against feeling too much. As she made him ache, he hated that she could wield that power over him.

"Mariah, I haven't been with a woman since I was with you. If you make me feel too good too soon, you're the one who'll be disappointed."

"Never," she said with so much feeling he had to smile. Then she added, "And if it happens fast for you, I'll get my turn later."

At that, he laughed out loud and pulled her to him for a kiss that told her more primitively than any words how much he desired her. Eventually he tore away and murmured, "You touch me however you want, and I'll keep what you said in mind."

She smiled, slid her hand up his chest, and lifted her lips to his for another kiss.

Her eager response made him harder, completely ready for her. But was she ready for him? He passed his hand over her hip, slipped it between her thighs. Her soft moan and arch toward him pleaded for more.

He stroked her, daring into intimate territory, wanting to give her pleasure like she'd never known. The first time hadn't been all pleasure and this time...

Her hands searched his body and stroked his skin in response to what he was doing to her. When her nails dug into his backside and her heat melted around him, he knew she was as ready as he was. But he was still worried about her being pregnant.

Wrapping his arms around her, he rolled to his back, pulling her on top of him. "Ride me, Mariah. I want to make sure I don't hurt you."

Her eyes were passion-glazed but widened at his request. With her hands on his shoulders, she raised up, then slowly embraced him with her body. Jud let out a groan and reined in his need to thrust hard and fast.

But she must have sensed his control was hanging by a thread because she arched, then contracted around him saying, "Let go, Jud. I want this as much as you do."

He couldn't let go. If he let her see the extent of his desire and need, she could use it against him. He still wasn't sure if she'd married him for security and what he could give her or because she cared about him for who he was. He might never know, and he had to live with that. But he could guard himself from feeling too much while he did.

Relying on discipline he'd honed since he was a teenager, he measured the pace, giving them both pleasure. It wasn't until Mariah cried out his name that he found release.

In the aftermath, he realized that just like the last time with her, his climax had been shattering. This woman rocked his world, and he couldn't seem to make it steady again.

All the while holding her, he rolled to his side.

She opened her eyes and smiled at him. "That was wonderful." As if words weren't enough, she placed a tender kiss on his shoulder.

Still joined to her, his body quickened.

When she felt it, her smile became wider, expectant.

Running his thumb over her flushed cheek, he said, "You aren't used to this. Maybe we should wait before—"

She took his face between her hands. "Stop worrying about me so. I want to enjoy our honeymoon night as much as you do."

The feel of her fingers on his face was almost more intimate than other stroking she'd done. It stirred up a well of emotions that had stayed deep and buried for years. He covered her hands with his. "How do you feel about taking a trip with me?"

"To the stars?" she teased.

He chuckled. "No, to Forth Worth. The Summer Classic starts in a week or so and we all go. Mack,

Ted, Randy and I compete. Flo goes to be with Mack. My dad meets up with old friends. If we make the cuts, we'll be gone for two weeks.''

"I'd love to watch you compete."

"Other owners and Shelby will be there, too."

When Mariah was silent a few moments, he wasn't sure how she was going to react or even if she might pull back. It had been stupid to bring this up now. But he'd been thinking about more privacy, more nights in a hotel room where they could shut out the world.

Finally she gave a little shrug. "So Shelby will be there. I imagine if she wins, you'll get recognition as her trainer."

"That's how it works. Next to the Futurity in December, this is the most important event of the year for cutting horses and their trainers. It's not only the prize money, but, like you said, furthering the reputation of the Star Four."

"It'll be fun."

He'd never really thought of the trip as fun before. But one look at Mariah's face and her eagerness to experience something new told him this time could be different. Setting his lips on hers, he didn't think about competing, but about a trip to the stars.

Humming a Reba McEntire song Wednesday afternoon, Mariah went to the barn to hang up halters she'd used. Since her wedding night with Jud, it seemed all she wanted to do was sing or smile. She knew he was still holding back, she knew he was still guarding himself, but she was hoping if she loved him enough, that would change.

Before they'd come back to the ranch Sunday, he'd taken her to the Municipal Rose Garden and then out to dinner. They'd talked about their trip and everything he had to do to get ready. When they'd returned to the Star Four, Luke, Christopher, Jenny and Thatcher had been sitting on the porch and greeted them with good-natured joking. Mariah had felt part of a caring family and she liked the feeling. Missing her mother the way she did, the sense of kinship helped.

After their guests had left Monday morning, she'd moved her clothes and belongings into Jud's room. Their days hadn't changed much but their nights sure had. No matter how often Shelby's doubts played in her mind, she couldn't believe Jud had only married her to have legal rights over his child. And as far as her lack of experience in the bedroom, Jud was careful with her—she felt his restraint even when he climaxed—but he seemed to be enjoying himself as much as she was. Was she deluding herself?

Refusing to let Shelby Vance's jealousy ruin a beautiful day, she opened the barn door and went inside. Randy raised his hand in a wave as he led a roan mare from her stall. Mariah waved back and headed for the tack room.

As she rounded the door, she saw Thatcher, bent over, his arm slung atop a saddle hanging on its rack on the wall.

He pushed a small vial into his shirt pocket.

Tossing the halters aside, she rushed to him. "Thatcher, what's wrong?"

He straightened and gave her a faint smile. "Just a cramp in my thigh, is all."

Sweat stood on his brow and she suspected he was lying. "I'm going to get Jud."

Grabbing her arm, he bellowed, "No!"

"Thatcher…"

"I'm fine. Really. Jud has enough on his plate. We're not gonna bother him with a little cramp. Old age is just setting in sooner than I want it to."

"You need to see a doctor."

Thatcher released her arm and pulled himself up to his full height. "Don't panic on me, Mariah. I have an appointment the second week in August. He's a busy man. I'm not gonna call him with every little ache and pain."

Her father-in-law looked pale, and she wasn't convinced. "That's after the Summer Classic. Don't you want to get checked out before you go?"

Thatcher picked up a saddle blanket. "I'm thinkin' about not going."

"You don't want to see Jud compete?"

"He'll do better if I'm not watchin'. I'll help the hands keep an eye on things here."

She wasn't sure what to say to him or what to do.

Carrying the blanket to the door, he stopped. "Mariah, my little cramp. It's just between me and you. There's no reason to tell Jud. Agreed?"

When she didn't answer, he prodded. "I want your word that you won't tell Jud. Not before he leaves."

She didn't like making this promise. But Thatcher was as stubborn as his son. Even if she told Jud, and Thatcher refused to go to the doctor's, he'd be worried and his mind would be on his dad rather than what he had to do in Fort Worth. "All right. I won't tell him. But I want *your* word that if you have another 'cramp', you'll call your doctor."

Thatcher frowned. "You drive a hard bargain."

"I have no choice living around all these hard-headed males."

With a shake of his head and a crooked smile, he muttered, "All right. It's a deal. Now let's both get back to what we were doin'."

She watched him walk through the barn, his gait strong and sure. Maybe she couldn't tell Jud about the "cramp" but she felt she should tell him something.

Finding time alone with her husband was practically impossible so she decided to wait until they retired for the night. All through supper, Thatcher had caught her eye, as if reminding her of her promise. Jud had returned to the arena afterwards, and as she waited for him in their room, she wondered how she could keep her promise and do what was best for Thatcher at the same time.

She'd just showered and slipped into her night-gown when Jud opened the door, frowning. When his gaze met hers, she asked, "What's wrong?"

After he pulled his wallet from his pocket, he laid it on the dresser. "Dad said he's not going to Fort Worth."

Her heart beat faster. "Did he say why?"

Jud dumped a few coins onto the china plate. "He says he's getting too old for all the excitement. He says he wants to stay here to keep his eye on the ranch. It's never been a concern before. I think he's feeling poorly and won't say so."

"Did you ask him?"

"You know dad. Claims he's fine. But he didn't move around much today."

"What are you going to do?"

Raking his hand through his hair, he said, "I don't know what to do. If I stay here, he'll raise Cain—"

"Let me stay."

Jud went still and silent. Then he asked evenly, "You think that will do any good?"

"It might. I can cook decent meals for him. You know if he stays alone, he'll go to the bunkhouse and eat everything he shouldn't. And if something is wrong and he needs care, I could get it for him."

With a tilt of his head, her husband studied her. "I

thought you were looking forward to going to Fort Worth.''

A remoteness that had almost disappeared the past few days colored his voice. Coming closer, trying not to let more distance stand between them, she said, ''I *was* looking forward to going. But how are you going to concentrate on winning prize money and drumming up business if you're worried about your dad?''

''That's the only reason you don't want to go?''

''What other reason could I have?''

''Maybe *you're* not feeling up to a two-week honeymoon.''

From a greater confidence she'd gained with marrying Jud, she touched the placket of his shirt. ''Have I acted as if I don't want a two-week honeymoon?''

Catching her hand, holding it in his large one, he answered her. ''No.''

There were still doubts in his eyes, and she wanted them gone. ''I'll miss you. But we have every night until you leave. And I think we'll both feel better if Thatcher's not here alone.''

His blue eyes flashed with silver desire. Releasing her hand, he rested his fingers on her waist and drew her close. When he kissed her, he probed and questioned and took for a good long time. She dug her fingers into his thick hair, trying to tell him how much she would miss him.

As he raised his head, he said, ''I *will* feel better if someone's watching over him.'' Then he pulled away from her. "Before we take this any further, I'd better get a shower."

He smelled male, of honest labor, and she was attracted to him just as he was. "You don't have to on my account."

With a look of surprise, he brought her to him again for a more demanding kiss, a kiss that led them straight to their bed.

The purple and white petunias along the side of the house bowed to the July sun as Mariah took a walk, missing her husband so much she now knew what "pining" meant. He'd been gone for five days. When she'd watched him drive away, tears had clouded her eyes. But she knew she was doing the right thing by staying.

The days before Jud left had been busy, and he'd been more preoccupied than usual with packing and organizing. At least she hoped that's what it was. He'd called once from Fort Worth to tell them he was settled in a room with Randy, and that he'd done well on the first go-around. She was hoping he'd call again to tell her he made the finals, to tell her he missed her. He hadn't said that yet. Forcing herself to believe he wouldn't succumb to any of Shelby's moves, she just looked forward to seeing him home again.

Thatcher had been taking it easy, so when he came around the corner of the house in a rush waving at her, she ran toward him. But he looked fine and when she came within speaking distance, he said, "Your Mama's on the phone. She said it's important."

Thanking him, she jogged into the house and picked up the phone in the kitchen. "Hi, Mama."

"Hi, honey. That Mr. Whitmore sounds like a nice man."

"He is. I can't wait for you to meet Jud and his father. Is something wrong?"

The few moments her mother paused signaled there was. "Mr. Hopkins is selling the ranch. Some Wall Street tycoon bought it and everything's happening real quick. The problem is I need some money. I hate to ask you, knowing how hard you saved for the baby, but I don't know what else to do since I don't have time to earn some before I have to leave. I found a waitressing job in town, but I need first and last months' rent for an apartment by August first."

"Oh, Mama, I spent a bit of the money a few weeks ago for something foolish and just yesterday I went shopping so I can make things for the baby. I only have a hundred dollars left."

"I don't know what I'm gonna do. The apartment's three hundred and fifty a month. It doesn't have any furniture...and then there's utility hookups and a uniform for work... Even going to the secondhand store, I'd need about two thousand dollars to get set up."

"Can't Mr. Hopkins lend you some money?"

"Honey, his creditors are all over him. Maybe I could just find a room somewhere."

"You need a permanent place to live. Let me think about this. I'll call you back tonight."

"It's not your worry. I'll figure something out."

"Don't *do* anything until I call you. Promise?"

"All right. I promise."

When Mariah hung up, Thatcher stood just inside the door watching her. "Your mama need something?"

"It's my problem, Thatcher."

He placed his hat on the rack and sat down at the table. "You're family now. Your problems are my problems. And don't think you're leaving this kitchen without telling me about it."

Now she knew how Jud felt about not wanting to upset his father. She didn't want to burden him, yet she knew his blood pressure would go up if she walked away. "Mama's losing her home. She has to be out by August first, and to get an apartment she needs first and last months' rent."

"She doesn't have a nest egg?"

Mariah paced back and forth across the kitchen. "Mr. Hopkins never paid her very much besides room and board for the two of us. And the past five years he lost money and didn't often do that. What I took in for sewing bought us clothes and any extras. I brought what we saved with me, but there's not much left. Maybe I could go into town to the tailor shop and see if they'd hire me."

"You know Jud wouldn't stand for that. Why don't you ask him for the money?"

She shook her head. "He already thinks I married him for what he can provide. This would prove it."

"He'd want to help your mama."

"Deep down, he'd resent it, Thatcher. I know it. And we're just starting to make some headway."

"Ask her to come live here for a while."

Grateful, Mariah covered Thatcher's hand with hers. "You really are a kindhearted man. But I don't think that's the answer." Jud already felt confined by living with his father. Having his mother-in-law in the same house wouldn't help.

"I know what you're thinking," Thatcher grumbled. "Maybe you two should build a place of your own. We've got enough land."

Better not to offer an opinion on that one, she thought. Only Jud and his father could figure out whether they could live under the same roof peaceably or if they needed separate quarters.

When she didn't respond, Thatcher said, "If you don't want to ask Jud for the money, I'll gladly loan it to you till you get up the nerve to talk to him about it."

Nerve wasn't what she needed. She needed the confidence that if she asked, her husband would understand she wasn't just using him. But she'd never run from a problem before and she wouldn't now.

"I'll call him tonight at his motel. It's better if we figure this out together."

Thatcher winked at her. "Smart girl. And if he gives you a hassle, you just hand the phone to me."

She was beginning to understand Jud's need for privacy. Asking Thatcher to intervene would cause more problems, not solve any.

Chapter Nine

When Jud inserted the magnetic room key into the door to his motel room and opened it, he found Shelby sitting on the chair by the window. "What are you doing here?"

"Randy gave me his key. He and Ted are going to meet us here in a few minutes to go for dinner."

Shelby was getting on his nerves. Every time he turned around she was at his elbow or under his nose. He was missing Mariah like crazy—her smile, her touch, her sassiness. And he was worried about his dad. The last time he'd called the ranch, Mariah had told him Thatcher was eating properly and she was watching him carefully. There was no indication he was feeling poorly.

But not even winning runs could keep his mind on

all the hoopla instead of Mariah growing bigger with his child and his father's health. He had to put a stop to Shelby's maneuverings and tell her to find herself a new trainer. "Look, Shelby, you and I need to talk. I don't think—"

The ringing of the phone cut him off. Before he could reach the one by the bed, Shelby picked up at the desk. After she answered, she handed it to him. "It's Mariah."

Scowling at Shelby, he said, "Hi, Mariah," and was met by silence. He cleared his throat. "Is something wrong with Dad?"

"No. He's fine. I thought you were rooming with Randy."

"I am. Shelby, Randy, Ted and I are going to dinner."

"Randy and Ted are there?"

Annoyed with Shelby for causing trouble, disappointed Mariah didn't trust him, he answered curtly, "No."

"I see."

"Mariah…"

Loud enough for his wife to hear, Shelby said, "If we're lucky, they won't show up and we can spend the night alone."

Ready to wring Shelby's neck, he said to Mariah, "This isn't—"

She cut him off. "I just wanted to wish you good

luck and tell you everything is fine here. Enjoy your dinner.''

And before he could smooth things over and tell her he intended to put Shelby in her place, his wife cut their connection. He could call her back, but he doubted if she'd talk to him or believe what he said. He'd have to handle Mariah face to face when he got home.

Turning to Shelby, he said, ''When we get back to Tyler, you find yourself another trainer.''

''You're not serious!''

''Mariah's my wife, and she's carrying our baby. You had no call to rile her or to try and interfere. Upset her again and you won't find a reputable trainer to take you on.''

''Jud…''

''Get out, Shelby.''

His voice must have carried enough of his anger to make her realize he was *very* serious. She went to the door and left without another word.

Tossing his hat on the dresser, he crossed to the minibar intent on finding something inside that would burn on the way down.

The rumble of trucks pulling horse trailers brought Mariah to the kitchen door late Monday afternoon, the day after the final event in the Summer Classic. Her thoughts and emotions had been in a whirl ever since she'd called Jud, and Shelby had answered.

She'd kicked herself over and over again for being so foolish as to hope Jud was satisfied enough being married to her to stay away from Shelby.

Of course, knowing Shelby…

That phone call had stirred up all Mariah's doubts and insecurities, making her wonder if her marriage had been a mistake. When Shelby had answered that phone, she'd decided she couldn't tell Jud about her mother and ask him for money. After she hung up, she'd accepted Thatcher's offer of a loan. Her mother needed the funds now, and they'd wired them to her. But already Mariah was having second thoughts.

Feeling the baby move, she laid her hand on her stomach. She'd gotten bigger the past two weeks. Jud might take one look at her and wish he was back in Fort Worth with Shelby. He'd called again a few days ago and told Thatcher he'd made the finals, but she'd been in the shower at the time and afterwards she hadn't been about to call him back and hear Shelby's voice again.

Not knowing how things stood with her husband, Mariah decided to start dinner instead of going to find him. He'd be busy unloading horses…cleaning out trailers. She wondered if he'd won any of the final events, but she'd find out soon enough. She'd capped strawberries, made a salad, shaved beef for barbecuing and was squeezing lemons for a fresh batch of lemonade when she heard Jud's boots on the porch. Taking a deep breath, she kept squeezing.

The screen door opened and shut, bags rustled, and still she didn't turn around. Suddenly he was standing very close behind her. She smelled the clean scent of soap.

"I'm home," he said, his voice deep and close to her ear.

Swallowing hard, she kept facing forward. They'd be much too close if she turned around. And if she looked at him and saw something in his eyes that told her he'd done more than go to dinner with Shelby...

She knew she'd have to leave the Star Four.

"Did you win?" she asked.

"Sure did. Along with the prize money, they gave me a belt buckle and the best saddle you'll ever find in Texas."

She could feel his body heat as he stepped even closer and braced an arm on either side of her. "What about the others?" she managed as her breathing became shallow.

"Randy and Mack did real well. We'll be getting lots of calls."

"And Shelby?"

"Turn around and look at me, Mariah."

Her heart pounded in her ears. "I can't. You're standing too close."

"Not nearly close enough," he muttered, but he stepped back, dropping his arms to his sides.

When she turned, she knew she had to meet his eyes. Several things surprised her. He wasn't wearing his hat, and his shirt was clean, with fresh wrinkles, as if he'd just taken it from his suitcase. His jeans were clean, too.

"I took a shower in the bunkhouse. I didn't want to come in here smelling like a horse."

"Why does it matter?" she asked, lifting her chin.

He eyed her for a long silent moment. Then he answered her. "It matters because I've been away for two weeks and I was hoping for a good kiss. But I can see that's not going to happen till we get something straight. Shelby Vance is history. I told her to find herself another trainer."

"Before or after you went to dinner?" She wanted the whole story.

Jud settled his hands on Mariah's shoulders. "We didn't go to dinner. Shelby is a spoiled woman who thinks she can take whatever she wants, simply because she wants it. I told her she had no call riling you or interfering in our marriage."

"You did?" Tears came to her eyes that she had trouble blinking away.

"I did. I made promises to you when we married. Promises I intend to keep."

"So you and Shelby—"

"I was there as her trainer, Mariah. That's it. Are we clear on that?"

Relieved, filled with renewed hope on where they were headed, she nodded. Then she linked her arms around his neck. "Did you say you'd like a home-coming kiss?"

With a crooked smile, he nodded. "I sure did."

She lifted her lips to his. When he pulled her to him, he opened his mouth over hers. Closing her eyes, she savored the touch of his lips, so glad he was home, so happy to be back in his arms. She forgot about Shelby and doubts and Thatcher's loan because she needed Jud's desire as much as she wanted his love. As she parted her lips, his tongue branded her as his, searching and stroking.

His tongue continued to seduce as his hands roamed over her shoulder blades, down her back, to her bottom. Bringing her as tight against him as he could, he aroused any hormones that weren't already spinning. Tearing his mouth from hers, he swept her into his arms and headed for the staircase.

She locked her fingers behind his neck and asked, "What about supper?"

"It'll keep," he said hoarsely. "No one's going to come looking until we tell them it's ready."

Telling herself she should be embarrassed because everyone on the ranch knew Jud's intentions, she realized she didn't care. This was her husband and he'd been away for two weeks. What they longed to do was perfectly natural.

Jud laid her on the bed and undressed her with an urgency that was exciting and arousing. When he stripped, she watched unabashedly, always delighted by the male beauty of his body. His gaze locked to hers and, as he came down beside her, she saw the primitive gleam of need that had arisen between them from the first moment they'd met.

His hands touched her with the hunger of being deprived for two weeks. His kisses, wet and warm and long, urged their bodies together in a frenzied melding that tossed her to the highest cloud, whirled her into an ecstatic spin, then kept her floating until Jud's fast, furious release filled her heart with so much love she felt tears again prick her eyes.

When he cuddled her against him, she rubbed her cheek on his shoulder, glorying in the moment.

Abruptly pulling away, he kissed her on the forehead. "Don't go anywhere. I'll be right back."

She heard him gallop down the steps. A few minutes later, he brought in two large bags and set them on the bed. "Open them," he demanded, his eyes twinkling.

Pulling the first one toward her, she slid out the box, lifted the lid, and found a fine tan Stetson. With her throat tightening, she tried it on.

"Sure beats that straw thing one of the horses chewed," he said with a grin.

Leaning forward, she kissed him full on the lips.

But he pulled away. "Open the other one."

She hadn't seen Jud this relaxed since Montana. When she opened the second bag, she found a teddy bear dressed in denim, red kerchief and a cowboy hat. "Oh, Jud. He's adorable."

"Every kid needs a bear. And every kid needs a crib. How about tomorrow you and I go into town and outfit a nursery? We can use the room next door. We should be able to hear him. But we'll get one of those baby monitors, too."

"We really don't need everything for a few months," she teased.

With a smile, he laid his hand on her belly. "There've been changes since I've been gone. Soon *I'll* be able to feel him move. We should start getting ready."

Something had caused a change in Jud. Maybe it was the time apart. Maybe his heart was beginning to recognize feelings that had taken root in Montana. She knew she should tell him about Thatcher's loan. But she couldn't. Not right now. She didn't want to do anything to sever the bond she felt between them.

When he leaned forward to kiss her, she opened her arms to him again, the same way she'd already opened her heart.

Whistling, Jud climbed the porch steps, eager to have supper with Mariah, work for a while in the arena, then turn in early. But not to sleep. He stopped whistling and grinned. He couldn't seem to get enough of her or she of him. Maybe because they knew that in a few months circumstances would change with the birth of their child.

Yesterday they'd gone to one of those stores with everything just for kids and ordered a crib, changing table, baby bathtub, playpen and a smaller crib for downstairs. He'd wanted to buy bottles, but Mariah had told him she intended to breastfeed. Just the thought tightened his chest.

He'd also wanted to pick up everything else they'd need from diapers to rattles, but Mariah said she was sure there'd be more shopping trips before the baby was born. He'd kissed the teasing smile from her lips right there in the store. And then last night...

Mariah's hands and mouth on his body had taken him to a height of arousal he'd never imagined. Fighting for control had almost become a war he didn't care to win. Yet he couldn't let go with her completely. Pride or the need for self-preservation held him back.

Flo was rinsing berries at the kitchen counter when he stepped into the kitchen.

"Where's Mariah?"

The housekeeper smiled. "Down at my house making something for the baby. You might have to go get her. She forgets about time when she's sewing."

"I'm going to wash up and change my shirt first."

Upstairs, he took a clean shirt from the closet and noticed a few books on the floor inside the door. Mariah had told him she'd been to the library while he was away. The cover of the first book told him it was about raising children. The second...the second was a book on travel in the Caribbean. A slip of paper marked a page. When he opened it, he found pictures of Curaçao. That's where Christopher and Jenny had spent their second honeymoon. Was Mariah just curious about it?

The third book, with its castles and snowcapped mountains, urged readers to see the sights of France and Germany. Why was Mariah reading travel books? To feed her dreams? Or more than that?

Doubts he'd set aside nudged him. *She's young. She wants to see the world.* An old voice whispered, *Maybe she's planning on using you to do it.*

Unsettled, he washed up and changed his shirt, then went downstairs.

Thatcher was sitting on the sofa in the living room, reading the newspaper, his ankle crossed over his knee. "I took a call for you this afternoon."

Jud waited.

"A man over in Hillsboro heard about the Star Four's performance in Fort Worth. He has two yearlings for you to take on. Might want to buy a foal next year, too. Come Monday, he'll truck over his colts."

"You told him I'd take them?"

"Sure did."

"Why didn't you ask me first?"

With a rustle, Thatcher set the newspaper on his lap. "What's to ask?"

"Do you know how many calls I've gotten since I got back? Let alone owners who handed me their numbers in Fort Worth. I'm evaluating each one, deciding who we want to handle. You had no right to make this decision without consulting me."

His father's face reddened. "Why should I have to consult you? I *own* the Star Four."

"And *I'm* running it."

Thatcher rose to his feet. "I'd be runnin' it myself if my doctor would let me! You and everybody else seem to think I should be turned out to pasture."

"Even from the pasture you'd want to look over *both* my shoulders," Jud flared, his months of patience finally giving out. "Ever since I was a kid, you'd give me something to do, then second-guess me. If you want me to run this place, then let me do it!"

"I second-guess you to cover your tail. What if I give you control of the Star Four and you take off again?"

His father's lack of faith pressed a button deep inside that shot straight to a place that been hurting for years. "I don't think you ever *wanted* me to succeed...or stay. I think you've always wanted to rile me so I'd take off, and you could forget that I'm the reason my mother died."

Sweat broke out on Thatcher's brow as he bellowed, ''You're loco! You can't believe—''

Suddenly Thatcher clutched his chest and bent over.

''Dad. Dad!'' Jud rushed to his father, more scared than he'd ever been in his life. ''Flo,'' he yelled. ''Call 9-1-1.''

Mariah heard Jud's shout as she opened the door and her heart pounded. She ran into the living room and, seeing the stricken look on her husband's face as he laid Thatcher on the floor, she turned around and ran for the barns and more help.

The next hour became a blur as Randy and Mack came running with Mariah's call. Randy helped Jud give his father CPR until the paramedics arrived. They shocked him back to the land of the living, started an IV and rushed him away in the coronary care ambulance. Jud and Mariah followed, neither of them speaking. Mariah had never seen Jud so pale.

At the medical center, the paramedics pushed Thatcher into the emergency room, and Jud and Mariah had to wait in the lounge. It seemed like hours until a doctor spoke to Jud and explained his father needed immediate heart bypass surgery. After giving his consent, Jud guided her to another floor to wait.

And pray.

They'd no sooner sat down when he leaned forward in his chair, his hands clasped, dangling between his knees. "This is *my* fault. I never should have argued with him. I should have kept my mouth shut."

Realizing guilt as much as worry weighed heavily on her husband, she clasped his arm. "It's *not* your fault."

"It *is*." He pulled away, stood and paced. "You don't know what I said to him."

She couldn't stand to see Jud hurting so. Going to him, she looked squarely into his eyes. "It's not your fault any more than it's mine. I *knew* he wasn't feeling well. I found him in the tack room one day, sweating, looking bad. But he made me promise not to tell you because he wanted you to go to Fort Worth. It's why I suggested I stay home with him."

Jud's voice was raspy. "You should have told me."

"Maybe so. But what would you have done? Carried him to the doctor when he didn't want to go?"

"I'm not blaming you but—"

"Then don't blame yourself, either. It won't do any good. Our energy has to go into praying."

The nerve in Jud's jaw worked and his eyes grew moist. "If anything happens to him…"

She wrapped her arms around her husband and held on tight. They stood there a long time, holding each other, giving comfort to each other, keeping faith with each other. Eventually they sat on the sofa and held hands, needing the connection, praying for a miracle.

The hours passed slowly. Mariah called the ranch;

Jud fetched coffee for himself and milk for her. While she paged through magazines, then dozed on and off on his shoulder, he stared straight ahead, sipping the coffee, absorbed in his thoughts. She still hadn't told him about Thatcher's loan. The past few days had been so wonderful, Jud had been so much more relaxed and almost tender, she'd been afraid of spoiling it. And now...

Now she definitely had to wait.

When the surgeon finally appeared in the lounge, she and Jud stood.

"Your father is doing as well as can be expected. We performed a quadruple bypass. You won't be able to see him for a few hours and then only for a short while. So I suggest you go home and get some rest."

Turning to her, Jud said, "I'll call Mack to come get you. I'm staying."

The doctor began, "Mr. Whitmore..."

"I have to stay to make sure—" He stopped. "I have to see him as soon as I'm able. Even if he doesn't know I'm there."

She could see the determination in the slant of Jud's jaw and knew there was no point arguing with him. "All right. But forget about calling Mack. I'm staying with you."

"You have the baby to think about," he said firmly.

"You bet I do. And if I worry less being here with you, the baby will be better off, too."

Jud's gaze held hers for several moments, then he nodded.

The doctor gave them both the trace of a smile that told them he understood. "I'll have someone get you blankets and pillows."

As the surgeon walked away, Jud motioned down the hall. "I have to call Mack and tell him Dad made it through. I should call Luke and Christopher, too."

"He's going to be okay, Jud. You have to believe that."

"I'll feel better after I see him. I have to tell him I want him around to bounce his grandchild on his knee."

Without hesitating, she gave him another hug, wondering now if things would change between Jud and his father, if they'd have the chance to make them change.

When Mariah settled on the sofa beside Jud again, she fell asleep. Two hours later she awakened, her neck stiff from sleeping on his shoulder. His eyes were open.

He took a pillow from the corner of the couch and placed it on his lap. "Stretch out. You'll be more comfortable."

"You could stretch out, too, on the other sofa."

"I'm not going to sleep no matter how comfortable I am."

"You've been awake all this time?"

With a nod, he admitted, "I've been thinking."

Patiently she waited, giving him the chance to tell her more.

Shifting toward her, he played with the ends of her hair. "I might have been wrong about Dad all these years. I've been thinking about what you said—you know, parents wanting to protect their kids. And I've been playing over in my mind how I'd go about it." He paused for a moment, then continued. "Raising me alone couldn't have been easy for Dad. Maybe he criticized me and demanded and kept me in line because he wanted to teach me the best, give me the best, leave me the best."

"I think that's true," she said softly. "But you still have to decide if what he wants for you and what you want are the same."

Silence stretched a bit, till he responded, "Since we got married, I *have* decided. My dad wants to hand down to me a legacy worth having, a way of life, a future. And I want to do the same for my son or daughter."

"And if your son or daughter doesn't want it?" she asked, wondering if Thatcher and Jud would look at their children the same or differently.

"I'll figure out why, then stand back. If he or she wants to look around at other choices and would rather make a life somewhere else, the Star Four will still be a legacy after we're gone."

Love for her husband tightened her throat. "You're going to make a good father."

"Or die trying."

"No. You'll live trying. And so will Thatcher."

Jud tipped her chin up and kissed her with all the tenderness, gentleness and desire she wanted and more. When she settled on the pillow on his lap, she knew the J.T. she'd met in Montana and the Jud she'd found on the Star Four were becoming one and the same.

Soon she'd be able to tell him how much she loved him. And maybe soon he could tell her, too.

Chapter Ten

The moon was almost full, the stars twinkling bright against a black velvet background as Jud led Mariah into one of the old barns that was wood instead of metal. The brush of the hay under her sneakers broke the silence until she heard the swish of a tail and walked toward a dim light. This barn housed horses with injuries or problems monitored by the vet. Only three of the ten stalls were occupied.

Thatcher was well enough to leave alone now. A month after surgery, he was getting stronger day by day, taking longer walks, losing weight as he should have months ago. His brush with death had scared him into line and made him quieter. Something was different between him and Jud, but it wasn't something they talked about. Thatcher knew his son had saved his life. And Jud understood his dad's mind-set a little better. Still, they didn't seem to know how to act around each other without arguments spicing up their conversation.

Amazingly, Thatcher only stayed in the hospital seven days. For his first two weeks at home, Jud had slept downstairs on the sofa to be within calling distance. Things were working their way back to normal slowly as their preoccupation with Thatcher's health lessened.

Luke had visited his uncle last week and brought them an unusual wedding present—a double bedroll. Tonight, after Thatcher had turned in, Jud had pulled it from the closet, taken her hand with his blue eyes sparkling with desire, and brought her to the barn.

"What are we doing here?" she asked.

"It's a surprise," Jud answered.

The last stall on the right snagged Mariah's attention as a large, square flashlight glowed on a table in a corner. A pitcher of lemonade, a dish of tortilla chips, a bowl of salsa and another filled with strawberries sat next to it. The floor of the stall had been layered with fresh hay and quilts and blankets on top of them.

"You've been nursing Dad for the past three weeks. I thought it was about time someone did something nice for you."

Her voice stuck in her throat at his thoughtfulness.

"Flo's been doing as much as I have," she finally managed to say.

"Maybe. But I also thought we deserved a little privacy."

It did seem like someone was always around. Even last week when Jud had returned to their bed, Luke had stayed a few days, and they were aware of him on the same floor as they were.

Unrolling the bedroll, Jud unzipped it and laid it on top of the blankets.

"Luke never did say why he gave this to us. But I saw him wink at you. Something private?"

Jud shrugged. "Not exactly. But one time after Luke introduced me to *his* type of woman, I told him she wasn't *my* type. I made some comment about wanting to be with someone who would like sleeping in a bedroll under the stars. I guess he thinks you fill the bill."

"Do I?" she asked, thinking maybe tonight was the night he'd tell her he loved her.

"Yes, you do," he said with a smile. "But I thought the ground would be a little hard in your condition. This'll be a lot more comfortable." Taking her hand again, he pulled her down to the bedroll with him.

Her "condition" was definitely getting rounder week by week, but it hadn't seemed to affect Jud's desire or hers. They undressed each other slowly, lingering, kissing long and deep, touching with the excitement of the first time, the adventure of a different place, the sensuality of summer and hay and night.

Ever mindful not to hurt her, Jud lay facing her. When they were both glistening with passion, he positioned her leg over his hip and entered her with care.

As happened every time, making love with him excited her, thrilled her and deepened her feelings for him. After they'd sated their passion, he kissed her temple and murmured, "Darlin', you always make me feel so good."

He'd never used an endearment before.

He was becoming more open with her...freer.

Feeling guilty because she hadn't told her husband about Thatcher's loan, she remembered the check from her mother that Thatcher had received yesterday. It was the first hundred dollars of repayment.

Maybe she didn't *have* to tell Jud about it.

As he tilted her chin up to kiss her on the lips, she pushed the loan out of her thoughts and whispered, "Thank you for tonight."

He responded by kissing her as if he loved her.

Feeling as if he owned the world, Jud rode his chestnut gelding to the main road to pick up the mail, letting the hot August wind dry his damp shirt. Randy usually rode to the mailbox, but today Jud had been checking fences and decided to go for it himself. The sky couldn't be any bluer or the sun any brighter. Not one cloud puffed across the blue. For the first time in a long time, he appreciated all of it.

After he took the mail from the box and mounted again, he glanced at the main road for any sight of the truck Mariah had taken to town. He wasn't surprised when he didn't see it.

They'd made love in the barn until close to two a.m., then snuck into the house like two kids on an illicit date so they wouldn't wake his dad. This morning she'd insisted on driving herself to town to the library. He'd wanted to take her, but she'd told him she'd be careful and make the trip a short one. Not wanting her to feel trapped on the ranch, he hadn't argued.

With an adjustment to the brim of his hat, he nudged the gelding into a lope till he reached the corral, then he dismounted and hitched him to the fence. Taking the mail into the house, he separated the personal envelopes from the business ones. Several were addressed to Thatcher. As he sorted those from the pile, he took them to his father's room.

His dad's desk sat facing the window. Jud crossed to it, intending simply to plop the mail in the corner. But as he glanced down, his gaze fell to Thatcher's bank statement unfolded on the blotter. A figure in the debit column caught his attention. Two thousand dollars—cash withdrawal. It was unusual for his father to take money from his personal savings account.

When he checked the date, he saw the funds had been withdrawn while he was in Fort Worth.

Knowing his dad kept a ledger with notations, Jud opened the top desk drawer and removed it. The book fell open to the last entry. A two-thousand-dollar withdrawal. On the line next to it, Thatcher had scrawled "Mariah."

Mariah?

Two thousand dollars?

While he'd been away?

Why had Mariah needed two thousand dollars? Why hadn't either of them told him about it? What in blue blazes was going on?

Doubts and suspicions clicked through his head as if glad to be back. Mariah wanted more than a father for her child. *Their* child, he amended angrily, picking up the statement again and staring at it as if it couldn't be true.

She'd kept his dad's condition from him.

So he'd go to Fort Worth and she could wrap his dad around her little finger? Hell, she'd done that the day she'd arrived.

He remembered the books on the floor of the closet. Maybe she was planning a trip. Before or after the baby was born?

Had she decided this wasn't the life she wanted? Had she driven into town by herself to see a travel agent?

All questions he couldn't answer till she got back.

He could go to his father for the answers. Thatcher had been sitting in the arena earlier. Spinning on his bootheels, Jud headed down the hall to the kitchen. But before he reached the porch, he heard the rattle of the truck Mariah had taken to town. Hurrying through the door, he let it slam behind him and strode to the shed as if the devil were on his heels.

The late morning sun reflected in the truck's back bumper as Mariah hitched her books to her left arm and closed the shed door with her right. The top book slid from her pile and landed on the stones. It was a book about the Fiji Islands. Over the years she'd read most of the travel books in the library in Billings. She'd found lots of different ones here. But even becoming immersed in the pictures of Curaçao, where Jenny and Christopher had enjoyed a second honeymoon, she'd realized dreaming of visiting exotic locales didn't appeal to her anymore. She loved her life here on the Star Four. As she picked up the book she'd dropped, she smiled. It was still nice to read about faraway places, though.

She heard the crunch of boots as she straightened and saw Jud coming toward her, his expression thunderous. Could he have had an argument with Thatcher? Although her father-in-law was still taking it easy, the doctors insisted he could be healthier than he'd been in years. That meant Jud didn't have to coddle him. Yet he had been, maybe because he'd almost lost him.

Today the peaceful spell might have ended.

"Where have you been?" her husband asked her.

Had he been out in the sun too long? "I told you I was going to the library."

His gaze fell to the books in her arm, the one she'd picked up. "Thinking about a trip?"

His voice was hard and cold as it had been when she'd first arrived. "No. What's wrong?"

"I want to know why you bilked my father out of two thousand dollars."

"He told you that?"

"He didn't tell me anything. I saw his bank statement and his ledger with your name after the withdrawal. Were you planning on skipping town and extorting more out of him if I wouldn't give it to you?"

She'd thought Jud had feelings for her, was coming to trust her and their future. How could she have been so wrong? How could she have believed he might love her? Too angry and hurt to open her mouth without starting to cry, she began to walk straight past him.

He caught her arm. "I'm talking to you, Mariah."

Jerking away, she took a deep breath. "You don't want to talk. You're condemning me without a trial! You want to believe the worst. Well, maybe I took the money and bought a diamond brooch. Maybe I bought you a Christmas present. Maybe I dropped it into a hole in the ground to save it for a rainy day. But whatever I did with it, you won't find out by treating me like a stranger instead of your wife. Honest to goodness, Jud. I've tried every way I know to show you how much I...how much I... Oh, never mind. You believe whatever you want. Questions are a world different from doubts. And I'm wondering if you have too many doubts to ever make this marriage work.''

This time when she walked away, he let her go. It was a good thing, too, because if he hadn't, she would have fought him like a wildcat.

She would *not* let him see her cry.

Something in Mariah's eyes had warned Jud he'd better not stop her...he'd better not touch her. But he needed answers, dammit, and he was going to get them. It took him a while, but he finally found his father walking by the yearling pasture. He told himself to go easy, he told himself his father was recuperating, he told himself he'd almost lost the man he'd finally realized had been the cornerstone of his life.

As soon as Thatcher saw Jud, he said, "You look like you wanna curse a blue streak."

"Why did you give Mariah two thousand dollars?"

Thatcher pushed back the brim of his hat. "Did you talk to her about this?"

"She wouldn't give me an explanation."

"Did you go after her like a blind bear lookin' for honey?"

"*Why* did you give her the money?"

"Because she was afraid to ask *you* for it!"

"That's no answer."

"It is if you're really lookin' for one. She knows you think she's searchin' for a golden egg. But for whatever reason, she fell in love with some cowboy who called himself J.T., and she thinks she can find that cowboy in you. I was beginning to think she could, too. But now I'm not so sure."

"You're not talking sense," Jud muttered.

Thatcher rested his hand on the fence. "You don't want to hear sense. Just like you don't want to really feel what's inside you. If you could admit you think the sun rises and sets in that young woman, she could have told you her mama was in a pinch. The rancher they lived with is selling his place. Edda got a job waitressin' but needed cash to set up an apartment."

"Edda needed the money?" A sick feeling rolled in Jud's stomach.

"That's what I said."

"But you'd written Mariah's name..."

"Mariah...her mother. What difference does it make? You know, Son, I think you'd better take a ride and do some thinkin'. Mariah's not goin' to stand for your mistrust much longer. She's got too much pride for that. So if you don't want to lose her, you'd better claim her."

"She's my wife!"

"If you want to *keep* her your wife, you'd better tell her what that means to you."

Jud couldn't remember the last time he'd taken his dad's advice. Right now a ride and thinking sounded like a good idea. "I'm going to head out to the north pasture. If anyone needs me…"

"I'll stand in till you get back." Thatcher's grin was a cross between smug and teasing.

Shaking his head, Jud started for the fence where he'd left his horse.

"Jud?"

He stopped.

His father's expression was more serious than he'd ever seen it. "I never blamed you for your mama's dying. For years afterward, I guess I was still mourning and missing her so much that that's what you thought. The truth is—you were the reason I kept going. You were the reason I made the Star Four what it is."

Since his father's surgery, Jud had wanted to tell him all the things he'd realized that night at the hospital. But the words still wouldn't come. So he walked back to Thatcher and carefully put his arms around him. "Thanks, Dad."

Thatcher cleared his throat and patted Jud on the back. "I'm proud of you, Son."

When they pulled away, there was an understanding between them. Jud took off to get his horse…and to come to terms with his marriage.

The leaves on the live oaks rustled as Jud brought his horse to a stop. He'd ridden hard past windmills, creosote posts stretched with barbed wire, stands of crabapple and hickory. Cattle lowed in the distance. Ducks quacked, and from the rise he saw grass rolling in the wind, gleaming almost silver in the sun.

His offspring would be the keeper of all this some day. And somehow that fact didn't mean as much as his marriage and his feelings for his wife. He'd been fighting the bit of caring-too-much-too-fast since he'd first met Mariah. Her green eyes, her smile, her shining auburn hair had grabbed his attention and wouldn't let go. But even more than her beauty, he'd been attracted to her spirit, her curiosity, her enjoyment of life.

He'd fought the attraction tooth and nail and lost the battle that night in the barn in Montana. He'd lost the war the day Mariah had appeared in the Star Four barn and told him she was pregnant. But the way he'd grown up hadn't taught him to acknowledge softer feelings or to separate them from desire.

When he looked back over the time since she'd arrived, he realized his doubts about Mariah had more to do with himself than her. He'd doubted his own worth, his ability to care deeply, to trust…to love. Love. What a frightening word filled with a world more immense than duty or responsibility. Love asked and pushed and demanded, not the minimum—but the best. He'd been afraid to give his best because it meant tearing down fences he'd spent years constructing. It meant putting his heart into Mariah's hands. It had been safer to believe she wanted to use him rather than love him.

But he knew better now. When he considered how she'd accepted him, orneriness and all, how she welcomed him with her body, how she cared so deeply for their unborn child as well as his father, he saw her love.

He knew he loved her.

And it might be too late.

What if he'd killed her feelings for him with his suspicions...with his lack of trust? What if she'd had enough of his doubts, and her pride made her leave?

He swore, took up the reins and nudged his horse into a lope, then a dead run. Riding hard, scenery flashed by as he raced against time, finally taking his mount right up to the house.

After he jumped out of the saddle, he called to a hand across the lane, "Cool him, will you?" Then he tore inside, letting the screen door slam behind him, and called, "Mariah!"

No one answered him and he panicked. He checked every room on the first floor, then took the steps two at a time. When he entered their bedroom, he saw she wasn't there, either. With an oath, he flung open the closet door. Her clothes hung beside his. She wouldn't leave without her clothes, would she?

He found himself checking the shed. The truck she'd driven hadn't disappeared, and it suddenly dawned on him where she could be. Taking off for Flo and Mack's house, he prayed she'd be there.

When he knocked, Flo opened the door. "I suppose you want to see Mariah?"

"She's here." He breathed a sigh of relief.

"I'm not sure I should let you in. I've never seen her cry before—not even after her showing up here pregnant and you acting like a bronc with a burr under his saddle blanket."

Guilt ate at him, deeper than any he'd ever felt. "I won't upset her more."

Flo gave him a thorough once-over. "All right. You never lied to me. Go on in."

Following the hum of the sewing machine, Jud found his wife easily. He hadn't been in Flo's sewing room for years. The noise of the machine should have hidden the sound of his footsteps, but when he crossed the threshold, Mariah's back stiffened as if she'd sensed his presence. Looking over her shoulder, she took her foot from the control pedal.

Frozen for a moment, not sure of what to say or do, he was afraid she'd turn away. "Mariah," he said in a husky voice that didn't sound like his.

The chair was on rollers, and she swiveled around to face him.

"I was afraid you'd left," he said.

"I'm carrying your child, Jud. I wouldn't leave without telling you."

He could see the evidence of tears on her cheeks, and his chest became so tight he could hardly breathe. "You left once before."

"That was before we married."

"Marriage does make a difference, doesn't it?"

Her voice quivered slightly when she replied, "I'm not sure it has with us."

Crossing to her, he snagged a straight-backed chair and sat with his knees nudging hers. "Yes, it has. It's made me realize that I want to live with one woman the rest of my life."

"Live with?" she repeated, her cheeks gaining color. "Is that what you think marriage means? Living with someone because it's convenient? Because you're sure you'll have someone to warm your bed and meet your needs?"

He knew he deserved her anger. He'd done nothing to deserve what he wanted most—her love. "Is that what you think I want?"

"I don't know what to think anymore," she said, turning away and looking out the window.

"That's my fault," he murmured, not sure how to say what needed to be said, not sure how to ask her for forgiveness. If he charged ahead without doing this right, he was afraid she might leave...for good. "Mariah, I know I've been ornery and stubborn. I haven't done anything much to make you want to stay. But I need you here with me. I want to be married to you.''

Her eyes grew wide and wary as her gaze met his again. ''You married me because of the baby.''

''No! I mean, yes, the baby pushed things along, but I married you because of you.''

As if she couldn't believe him, she shook her head. ''You've never said you felt anything for me. You certainly don't trust me—''

He so badly wanted to take her in his arms and forget about finding the right words. But Mariah needed to hear the words as much as he needed to say them. ''I didn't trust myself. I didn't trust my heart. I was trying to stay safe by denying what I felt, by pretending you weren't as important to me as our baby. And I've given you plenty of cause to drive down that lane and never look back.'' Stopping, he turned phrases over in his mind. Then giving up on finding the perfect one, he forged ahead. ''Hell, Mariah, I'm not any good at pretty words. But I love you.''

She blinked for a moment. Then, flipping off his hat and dropping it to the floor, she said, ''I don't want a shadow on your face. Say that again.''

With his heart pounding, he took her hands and brought them to his lips. After he placed a kiss on both, he repeated, ''I love you. I don't want to live without you. I want to make more babies with you and grow old with you. And if you can forgive my doubts and how mule-headed I've been—''

"Can you forgive me keeping the loan from you? I never meant to. I was just so afraid…''

As he drew her to her feet, he enfolded her in his arms. "No more fear. No more doubts. Just forgiveness and trust and love." His lips met hers and, when she opened to him, he kissed her with every bit of passion and feeling in his heart.

Eventually raising his head, he murmured, "You haven't said it yet."

Mariah took Jud's face between her hands, seeing a vulnerability and openness that had never been there before. "I love you, Judson Thatcher Whitmore. And if you ever hide behind that tough cowboy facade again, I'll know my J.T. is in there somewhere."

Smiling, he promised, "That tough cowboy is gone forever. You've changed me, Mariah."

She wrapped her arms around his neck and lifted her lips for another kiss. This cowboy was hers—for keeps.

Epilogue

The church's stained glass windows splashed colors on the sanctuary's carpet. As the scent of pine from wreaths, the flicker of candlelight on the altar and the manger scene set off to one side proclaimed the coming of Christmas only a few days away, Mariah rocked Daniel Judson Thatcher Whitmore. Jud's arm curved around her shoulders as the minister pronounced the final blessing. They'd planned the christening close to Christmas so that Christopher, Jenny and Luke could share this special day as well as the holiday with them. They'd asked all three to be three-week-old Daniel's godparents.

The family standing around the baptismal font would be so important to this child's life, Mariah mused. Jud had insisted her mother fly in for the birth of their son and stay with them as long as she liked. Thatcher had seconded the motion. Thatcher and Edda had kept company since the day her mother had arrived and, from the way they looked at each other, Mariah suspected more was blooming than friendship.

Flo and Mack stood next to Luke, with Randy, Ted and the other hands beside them. The joy swirling around Mariah brought her cheek to the top of her son's head as tears misted her eyes. The minister smiled and congratulated them on the christening of their son.

Jud lifted her face toward him and kissed her.

Christopher nudged him. "This is a christening, not a wedding."

Jud's face flushed. "We take advantage of the moment whenever we can."

Luke chuckled. "I saw you two sneak out to the barn with a flashlight last night."

Mariah had asked her mother to watch the baby for a few hours while she and Jud spent some time alone. She hadn't thought anyone else had known they'd left the house. But Luke had decided to bed down in the bunkhouse since one bedroom was now a nursery and the guest rooms were filled. He must have still been awake when she and Jud had sought privacy in the barn.

"Were you sitting up making your Christmas list?" Mariah teased. Ever since her talk with him about Jud, he'd almost become a big brother.

"Nope. I don't want anything this year," he answered with a smile.

Daniel made a gurgling sound and lifted his arms into the air. The look on Luke's face as he gazed at her son contradicted his words, as did the tender way he'd held and handled his godson since he'd arrived.

Leaning close to Luke, she suggested, "I think you're afraid to make a Christmas list because your heart might tell you what you really want."

His green eyes became serious. "You could be right."

Jenny tapped Mariah's arm. "Can I hold Daniel for a few minutes?"

"Sure you can." Mariah handed over her precious bundle.

Jud whispered in her ear, "I think Christopher and Jenny are practicing to be parents."

"It's an awesome responsibility," Mariah murmured.

Circling her with his arm, Jud agreed, "Yes, it is. But with the love we have for each other and all these people behind us, we can't help but succeed."

Her cowboy talked about love more freely now, along with showing it. She laid her head against his shoulder, thankful for his strength, his integrity, his honesty with himself and with her that urged their marriage to grow stronger day by day.

When he brushed his cheek against her temple, she knew happiness so great it could last for years.

His lips grazing her brow, Jud said, "We're blessed."

"Yes, we are," she responded, knowing her husband's love would always be the greatest blessing of all.

* * * * *